# Love
# and
# Protest

# Love
# and
# Protest

A Novel

By Nancy Klann-Moren

AnthonyAnn Books

LOVE AND PROTEST: Copyright@2024 by
Nancy Klann-Moren

AnthonyAnn Books


ISBN: 978-0-9884944-4-2

Cover Design: Ron Larson

This is a work of fiction. With the exception of the public figures connected with the current and historical events mentioned in the story, the principal characters are all fictitious and the product of my imagination.

www.nancyklann-moren.com

For my husband, Richard,
who brought light and laughter
into my life.

*"The biggest victory is that we did fight...*
*That we came together and we fought.*
*And that we have that history to build on."*
                              *~ Kipp Dawson*

# 1

## Harper

## May 15, 2019

I'd been walking through the streets of Hickory Springs for over an hour when a honeysuckle vine caressing the sign above a small shop caught my attention. I'd been to the place a couple of times before and never took to heart the words those slender stems embraced—*Second Chance Thrift Shop*.

The affectionate way the vine held onto the sign caused me to open the door and step inside. The little bell overhead rang out with an arrogant clatter to make my arrival a big deal.

It was only mid-May, but the humidity had turned as thick and rank as a Georgia day can hand out. The air conditioner buzzed with conviction but did little to cool the place.

Through the haze of artificial light, an old woman sat behind a desk near the back wall. Her snow-colored updo sagged from the heat. She smiled and flashed a set of extra large dentures. With every ounce of Southern charm she had to give, she said, "Oh, darlin', I just love your hair. I always wanted to be a redhead."

Instead of getting into a conversation about how much teasing goes along with having red hair, I said, "Thank you."

"Furniture and glassware are half-price today. Green tags are discounted twenty-five percent, and everything upstairs is on clearance."

Even though I didn't have money, I gladly climbed the stairs to the second-floor loft to escape the possibility of more chit-chat. Each step took its turn in a symphony of creaks and groans and chirps until I reached the landing.

Gloomy shadows loitered over the odds and ends that had previously had their moment to shine downstairs and, after some time, were relocated and discounted.

Against the side wall, next to a grandfather clock that had lost its hour hand, stood a nightstand covered with a thick blanket of dust. As I puckered my lips and blew on the dust, a streak of light entered from a small dormer window, highlighting the gleeful dance of the liberated particles.

The clear glass knobs on the two drawers glistened like the crystal pendant Mama wore on special occasions. When I pulled on the top knob, the drawer opened about two inches and jammed. I pulled harder. It released with a jerk and slid smoothly.

Toward the back was a faded, leather-bound book with a locking clasp and gold, fancy writing on the cover. It said, *Diary*. The cracks at the corners and the worn, discolored surface made me wonder how old it was.

On the first page, handwritten in blue ink, it said, "Property of Libby Carlson." My skin tingled as I flipped past something called a prefatory, straight to the entries.

> January 1, 1967—Sunday.
> *I'm a Believer. The Monkeys. New year, new start, new song, or better yet, my new philosophy. No more being the one left behind. No more disapproving parents. 1967 will be my year of action. I'll be with Rachael in SF for my 18th in fourteen days. The planning begins tomorrow morning.*

> January 4, 1967—Wednesday.
> *4 days until I leave. My plan is coming together. I stayed up until 3 in the morning, getting things ready. I've been sneaking around the house like a burglar, but fingers crossed, my folks don't suspect anything. I'm leaving Sunday—the first day of my freedom.*

Turns out we're both Capricorn babies. Three days apart. My birthday is the seventeenth.

The ink on the pages looked like a delicate blue thread set free from its spool, revealing Libby's feelings and plots.

Almost seventeen and a half, and I'd never jotted down my thoughts into a book and trusted it to protect them.

Clutching it against my chest, I felt its heartbeat, its need for rescue, and the destiny of my day.

"You doin' okay up there, sweetie?" the lady yelled from downstairs.

"Yes, thank you. Almost done looking."

I slipped Libby's diary into my backpack and went down to the first floor, feigning interest in a box of old Victorian greeting cards. I smiled at the woman and waved goodbye, then stepped through the door with the little bell broadcasting my departure and the promise of discovering more about the girl whose diary hitched a ride in my backpack.

The clouds thickened as I slogged toward home thinking about Libby Carlson leaving one place and starting over in another. I couldn't get past the second-chance connection. *I wish Mama had a second chance.*

Prospect Avenue, a once thriving part of town, had fallen on hard times. I walked past an abandoned cottage with murky windows and a single-wide on cinder blocks. Across the street, a chain-link fence surrounded the abandoned building that was once the Piggly Wiggly. The twenty-foot faded logo of a cartoon pig smiled from the brick wall.

The seam on my right sock dug into my baby toe. I sat on the bus bench to smooth it out. A patch of dried-up swamp lilies pushed through a crack in the sidewalk next to me. At first, I admired the way they made the best of their situation until I realized they were barely holding on to life and sad like me.

The old grocery store was the very place Mama and I used to shop together each week. Her voice came to me as if she was there. "Harper, you collect the fixins for breakfast, and we'll meet over by the fresh corn, then go down the cookie aisle together."

A metal clip on a flagless pole clanked in the breeze, bringing me back to the present. When cars drove past, old, discarded plastic bags thrashed against the fence, and I watched them flounder.

I grabbed the diary from my backpack, set it on my knees, and ran my hand over the nubby cover. Unlatching the clasp again, I fanned past the few pages I'd already read.

> January 6, 1967—Friday.
> *I'm completely packed and jumpy as a cat, waiting for my folks to catch me red-handed in my plans to leave. Not sure if they'd really care. Not sure they ever have.*

January 7, 1967—Saturday.

*Bye-bye shoveling snow and slick roads. Bye-bye land of 10,000 nasty mosquito bites. Bye-bye, Minnesota, and hello to the rest of my life. Route 66 West, a week to get to SF for my 18th with Rachael!!! I'm ready and leaving tonight. 3 am, to be precise.*

I admired the guts it took to decide her own destiny without knowing what was next. And the idea of being someplace, anyplace, where her past wasn't a barrier to people's perception of her tugged at me.

She would have been six months older than me when she wrote these entries. The idea there was a better place beyond the deteriorating town of Hickory Springs hadn't ever before held the kind of weight it did that day.

Sitting on the bus bench, Forest Gump-like, my head bounced with random thoughts. *Would I be able to write something in a diary every day? No. Would reading someone else's diary be considered snooping? Yes. Would I want some stranger from fifty years into the future reading my shit? Hell no. But how could I not?*

What if I treated it like a box of chocolates and slowly satisfied my curiosity by reading one or two entries at a time? It would be less snoopish. My hand stroked the front cover, and I said, "I swear to you,

Libby Carlson, no one will know about this except you, me, and Mama."

I hadn't paid for the diary, and I hadn't actually stolen it either. There was no price tag, which I took to mean it had come to me as a gift from the universe—or something Mama had guided me to find on a down in the dumps day. Even though she'd been gone four months and seven days, she had a knack for looking after me.

A white Pest Away Pest Control truck drove by as slowly as if its engine had stalled. The driver rolled down the window and whistled at me, high-pitched, like he was calling for a stray dog.

"Hey, Carrot Top, you want a piece of this?" His beady eyes and crooked smile guaranteed my answer came in the form of a middle finger.

He laughed and returned the gesture, then gunned his engine. A nasty, chemical stench filled the air. The blood rose in my cheeks. Sometimes, the burden of having red hair seemed unfair.

# 2

On my sixteenth birthday, a year and a half before I found Libby's diary, Mama got up early.

"Harper, Darlin', she hollered from her bedroom, "I'm starting with the breakfast shift today. I'll be done by the time you get out of school, and we can get on the road then."

Ever since I turned ten, we drove sixty miles north on Highway I-75 to celebrate my birthday at The Southern Belly. I cherished our yearly excursion and considered it the third best day of the year, after Christmas and Fourth of July.

We'd sit in a padded booth and share an order of tender pork ribs with collards, onion rings, and a pickle spear. We pulled the ribs apart, ate the meat off one side, turned it over, and finished it off before licking it clean. To top off the meal, we each had our own deep-fried brownie supreme. Mine had a candle.

Not forty-five minutes into my first class, Miss Dixon told me, along with the all the other kids, the principal required my presence in her office.

When I got there, Mrs. Adams said, "Just give me one minute to finish this filing. Have a seat, Harper."

"What's wrong?" I knew I hadn't sworn at anyone, like the last time she called me in.

Mrs. Adams closed the file, then turned around.

"We got word that your mother took a fall at work, and Mr. Boon drove her to Hickory Springs Memorial. He's coming here to pick you up and take you there."

"Who's Mr. Boon?"

Her face twisted. "LeRoy Boon, her boss at The Blue Rooster."

In all the time I'd known him, I'd never heard LeRoy's last name.

"What happened?" I nervously tugged on my braids.

"I didn't get the details, but he'll be here soon." She brushed a small strand of paper off her skirt.

When LeRoy entered Mrs. Adams' office, splotches of blood were on his chef's apron. I jumped from the chair.

"What happened? Is Mama okay?"

"She'll be fine."

"Is that her blood?"

He looked down. "Sorry. Didn't realize I still had this on."

"What happened?"

"She took a bad spill." His shoulders slumped. "It was the first order of the day. I set two stacks of hotcakes on the pick-up station, and she put them on the serving tray with all the fixings for the order."

"What happened? Jeeze, LeRoy, I don't care about the order. Tell me what happened."

"Sorry. She slipped on a puddle of water, and the tray flipped ass-over-teakettle. She tried to catch her fall by grabbing hold of a table but missed and went down on her elbow."

"Good Lord," Mrs. Adams said.

"What about the blood?" My eyes didn't leave LeRoy's apron.

"One of the plates broke when it hit the floor." He untied the drawstring and took off the apron. "Some of the shards hit her leg. Superficial cuts. Nothing to worry about. But I think she might have shattered her elbow, and I know she busted a couple of fingers on her right hand."

"Was she crying? Will she be okay?"

He rolled the apron in a bunch and tucked it between his arm and ribs. "No, she didn't cry. She was brave and held her breath when me and some of the regulars wrapped her arm and got her into the truck. The folks in the emergency room are taking good care of her. Come on, let's get you over to the hospital. It's a ten-minute drive from here."

"They're prepping her for surgery," the woman behind the reception desk said. "The waiting room is on the third floor. Elevators are straight ahead."

As soon as we arrived at the waiting room, LeRoy said, "Wish I could stay, but we're short-staffed."

"What? You're leaving?"

"Don't worry. She'll be fine."

"Are you coming back?"

"Of course, if I get a break."

A grid of sad, beige panels hung from the low ceiling. The one above the entrance had a big, dirty water stain, the shape of Florida or maybe Italy.

Plastic chairs lined the walls. I sat in one at the back, feeling abandoned and scared, hoping the hospital did a better job taking care of the patients than it did the family members.

A brown sign next to the light switch said, "Waiting Room." A row of nubby Braille symbols stretched under the words. I couldn't help but walk over, close my eyes, and run my fingers across the raised dots. *How do blind people even know there's a sign there?*

Switching from one chair to the next, I watched the second hand on the clock move forward in small jumps.

The scratchy voice on the overhead public announcement system called out instructions to the staff. *Code blue, second floor. Code gray. Dr. Sinclair.* And a whole mess more.

Each time it squawked, my heart jumped, and my brain worried that the codes might be about Mama. To make things worse, I swear I heard my name called out three separate times.

It was no secret how I got the name. *To Kill A Mockingbird* was Mama's favorite book since she first read it in the sixth grade. It served as her handbook for how to do right in life. Whenever she could fit one in, she'd quote phrases from the book to make her point or teach a lesson.

"Atticus doesn't wear a cape or leap tall buildings," she'd say. "But he's the closest we have to a hero."

If he had been real, I'm sure she would have stalked him. One Christmas, she embroidered *What Would Atticus Do?* throw pillows as gifts.

I had no idea how long an operation took, but I knew I'd been alone for four hours, wondering how it could be that no one else had ever entered the room.

The hallway led to the bathroom, eighty-seven steps, door to door. After peeing, I walked up and back, up and back, bored to tears, surrendering to the uncertainty while listening to my shoes slap the linoleum.

Back in my chair, I picked up last July's *Country Cooking* magazine from the side table. I'd flipped through it earlier, but this time a recipe for Salt and Pepper BBQ ribs stopped me sure as if it had stabbed me in the heart.

A man smiling real big, like he'd just won the Mega Millions jackpot, held a wooden tray of meaty ribs basted with pan drippings. The recipe for "cooking them low and slow until the meat falls off the bone" was printed under the tray.

The salt from my tears burned my eyes. *We should have been on our way to The Southern Belly by now.*

I tore the page from the magazine and ripped it in half. Then, ripped those halves in half. Then again, and again, until the paper bits were so small, they dropped through my fingers onto the floor like unwelcome confetti.

*Where's Uncle Kevin? Why isn't he here? Didn't he know? Did LeRoy forget to call him?*

Our phone was somewhere in the hospital, in Mama's purse. But where?

Sharing a phone sucked. We lost our two-line plan because of late payments and had to get a prepaid. Mama kept possession of it on weekdays, saying I had no need for it in school.

A silver glint flashed off the stethoscope of the tall man who stepped into the room.

"Are you Ellie Warner's daughter?" He looked down at the ripped papers on the floor and frowned.

"Harper," I said. "Is she okay?"

He nodded. "I'm Dr. Hanson, her surgeon. The procedure lasted longer than expected but went very well."

I slumped in relief.

"You can see her when she gets out of recovery. Someone will take you to her in an hour or so."

My eyes darted to the clock—three minutes to four. *Another fucking HOUR?*

"Is her arm okay?"

"It will be. She shattered her elbow in ten pieces." I involuntarily winced. "We were able to align and secure them with the help of fourteen small titanium screws."

I pulled on my braids. "Fourteen screws?"

"Along with her wrist fracture and broken fingers, it's a lot. Having said that, she'll be released in three days and on the mend soon." He pulled a pager from his pocket and read the message. "If you'll excuse me, I need to take this."

At four-forty-five, an orderly poked his head into the room.

"What happened here? What's with the paper scraps on the floor?"

"Someone should clean it up."

"Are you Ellie Warner's daughter?"

I gave him a thumbs-up.

"Your mother's in room 343. I'll take you there."

Lagging behind, I studied how his bow-legged swagger tugged at the hang of his scrub pants. As he ushered me into her room, he said, "Just know, she's still under sedation."

On each side of the room were two beds. Directly across from Mama, in bed C, a pale woman slept with an oxygen tube stuck to her nose. Her open mouth reminded me of a baby bird waiting for food.

In Mama's area, a monitor beeped out warnings and flashed coded warnings. Her arm looked the size of a thigh wrapped in surgical gauze.

She tried to say something but struggled to push the words out. I leaned in to catch each jumbled syllable, but it didn't take long before she fell back asleep.

Her purse sat on the bedside table. I took twenty dollars and the phone, then called Uncle Kevin from the hallway.

"What?" he yelled. "This morning? Why didn't anyone call me? I'll finish up here but might not get there for an hour."

"All I had was a Pop-Tart before school. I'll be in the cafeteria."

The scent of pizza lingered as I slid my plastic tray along the stainless platform in front of the Plexiglas shield. Past the carrot raisin salad, the Jello cups, and the two types of soup, I grabbed the Mac 'n Cheese. A paper plate with three Chocolate Chip Cookies covered in plastic wrap looked like the best of the desserts.

*Happy fucking birthday to me.*

Despite the empty coffee cups on the table close to the television, I claimed it.

Mounted to the wall, The *Diners, Drive-Ins, and Dives* guy was leaving Jerry's Chowda Truck, cruising through Boston in his red convertible, and searching for the best seafood chowder in town.

My chair also had a view of the elevators. Anxious families and clusters of support workers went in and out with an assortment of worry on their faces. Each time one of the doors opened, I expected Uncle Kevin would be there.

Halfway through an episode of *Chopped*, he showed up and sat in the chair across from me.

"I stopped by Ellie's room but didn't have the heart to wake her." He rapped the table with his knuckles. "You ready?"

"Way beyond ready."

"Let's get rolling. You'll stay at my place tonight."


As promised, they released Mama on Saturday. Carrying a plastic bag stuffed with her personal items, I walked next to the nurse pushing her in a wheelchair to the sidewalk under the awning by the front door.

The nurse handed her a brochure on the benefits of ice and elevation and instructions on how to keep her cast clean. She also reminded her of her follow-up appointment and gave her a 30-day prescription for pain relief. 20mg of Oxycodone hydrochloride.

.

# 3

Flashes of pain hot as fire shot through the nerve endings in Mama's elbow, day and night. The Oxy had run out.

Figuring something went haywire during the operation, she went to the doctor's office to ask if they could schedule an MRI. Dr. Hanson assured her nothing went wrong with *his* procedure.

"We all heal differently. It will take more time for you." He reached for his prescription pad and scribbled out instructions for a more potent dosage of Oxycodone plus one refill.

Bridget, a girl in my school, got hooked on opioids. Megan and I watched her hide next to the bushes in the quad, picking scabs off her skin. We watched because of Mama's situation.

Megan and I met in the second grade when she and her mama came to Hickory Springs and rented a one bedroom in our apartment building. They had moved six times in two years.

On the same day they arrived, the Perfect Cuts Salon posted a help wanted sign in the window for a shampoo technician. They hired Megan's mom. She started work the following week. When Miss Rosie up and died three months later, she took over as a full-time beautician and has been there ever since.

Megan and I became fast friends. We held hands as we walked to school every day. She had a different hairdo each morning. When not down in loose curls, it was in a ponytail, a ballet bun, a topknot, or some other twisty thing locked into place with aerosol hairspray.

My simple braids never varied.

The story goes that her daddy died in the Iraq war. Unlike me, she ached for the chance to have known him.

I knew mine didn't marry Mama and left before I was born. I knew I was better off without that kind of person in my life. And I knew Mama loved me more than two people could. Even so, there were times when unspoken questions lingered.

The summer between the second and third grades, two giant cardboard boxes were left by the dumpsters behind our building. One said Kenmore washer and the other said Kenmore dryer.

We moved them between the buildings and converted them into a fort with a door and windows. We spent most of our time together there. Megan filled the walls with her hand-drawn doodles for wallpaper, and she painted flowers on the ragged pillowcases we used for curtains.

Inside the fort, we made up stories about our strong, handsome, pretend daddy's. Megan's had a mustache. Mine didn't. They both bought us bikes and taught us to ride them. We were all going to Disney World together, where they would hike us on their shoulders and parade us up and down Main Street. Our daydreams reached as far as two girls our age could stretch them until they felt stupid and heavy, and reality became easier.

When the rainy season washed our fortress away, our unrealistic fantasies of having two perfect families vanished with it.


Even though she couldn't work, Mama enjoyed spending her afternoons back at The Blue Rooster, talking up anyone who would indulge her in a conversation.

Being there wrapped her in the comforting scent of coffee and sang to her with the clatter of silverware tapping sturdy plates. And while there, she didn't have to look at our dining table cluttered with unpaid bills her disability benefits wouldn't cover.


By May, her arm began to heal and get stronger. So did her anxiety, paranoia, and need for Oxy.

Every time I saw her take a pill, I held my tongue about Bridget and her scabs because Bridget wasn't under a doctor's care like Mama.

When August rolled around, I finally decided to talk to her about it.

"Are you sure you need so many?"

"What?"

"Pills."

"I'm fine, Harper. Don't you go worrying about me."

While relieved with her answer, I continued to ask, until the day she snapped back, "Mind your own business. Stay out of my life."

A week later, she said something that never would have come out of her mouth if all was right. My mama, who loved me to death and beyond, answered, "I wish I'd never had you."

I withered into a petrified little girl who didn't know what to do. Oxy had taken my place.

I called Uncle Kevin to tell him.

"I just got off the phone with LeRoy. He said he had to ask her to leave the restaurant yesterday and not come back."

"Why?"

"I'm goin' over in a little bit to find out. I'll swing by to pick you up. We can both hear what he has to say."

Mama had worked for LeRoy more than eight years. He always said she was the best waitress he'd ever hired.

His big shoulders hunched when he saw us come through the door.

"Have a seat. I'll be right there."

He went to the prep station to talk with Pearl, one of the waitresses. She gave him a nod.

He lumbered over to the table, sat across from us, and shook his head.

"Thanks for comin'." He tugged on his earlobe. "Truth is, I haven't felt so bad about anything before. You see, I didn't grasp the real picture of what happened to Ellie, and didn't handle it so good."

Uncle Kevin rapped his knuckles on the table like he does. "It's okay, LeRoy, just tell us."

"Well, this is how it started. Ellie was sitting over there at that corner table by the storage closet and yelled to no one, 'You know, Harper Lee didn't write those words, don't you?'" He shook his head. "I mean, she yelled it out real loud." His eyebrows shot up. "Of course, I didn't know what she was talking about, but I walked over there and asked her to lower her voice."

LeRoy looked over at Pearl. "Can you bring us a pitcher of water and three glasses?" He folded his hands on the table.

"I told her it sounded like she was havin' a conversation with someone in Alabama. That didn't go over too well." He flashed a regretful smile. "Your mama narrowed her eyes and looked up at me, angry as a hornet. She said, 'Alabama? What the holy hell are you talking about, LeRoy? We're in Georgia, and this is important.'"

It didn't sound like something Mama would say, but LeRoy wasn't inclined to exaggerate.

"She was talking about Atticus Finch never saying something that was in the movie."

Pearl set the glasses on the table and poured the water from the pitcher. LeRoy took a drink.

"Then she shot up from the chair, causing it to fall backward. She seemed off balance, but her rant kept going. 'How about the man who wrote the movie keeps his voice down? Huh, how about it? He put words in Atticus' mouth that he didn't say in real life.'"

Uncle Kevin said, "I'm so sorry about this. It's the medication."

"Medication?" I said, feeling hopeless. "It's poison."

LeRoy said, "Yeah, she was pretty messed up. I was about to pick the chair up and set it right when she pounded her fist on the table and said 'What the fuck's wrong with you, LeRoy? Atticus never said those words.' And I had no other choice but to say, Ellie, you have to leave. I can't have you here anymore."

Right after Mama left the diner she drove her Hyundai to the Top Quality used car dealer and sold it for cash.

"Why would she do something like that?" I asked Uncle Kevin.

"Beats me, Harper. Maybe it's a weird form of penance."

"What's that?"

"Self-punishment."

"Or maybe she used the car money for more drugs."

The day finally came when she said, "Gotta get off this stuff. It's gonna be hard, but I gotta do it."

"Good, Mama. That's real good," I said, drowning in a puddle of guilt, certain she wouldn't have gotten so hooked if I had talked about my fears earlier.

"I might need your help, she said while tilting her head and squinting at me. "You took your braids out."

It had been three weeks since I got rid of the Little Red Riding Hood look, and she finally noticed.

I'd stumbled onto a blog that called out to me titled *Owning Your Redness.* Being a redhead made me feel like I was kind of weird, but reading about how only two percent of the world's billions of humans have naturally red hair helped me see it as special.

The more I read, the more I wanted to know, like the MC1R gene is responsible for our hair color and we're more susceptible to pain. The blog went on to say we symbolize magnetism and mysticism. It made me feel a teensy proud and good about something. The blogger encouraged us to let our ginger tresses fly, so I did.

Her nose and eyes ran nonstop. Her skin had become red and blotchy from all the scratching. She mostly kept to herself in her bedroom, on top of the bedcovers in her I FIGHT LIKE A GIRL pajamas.

Her legs twitched with spasms. When nausea consumed her, she leaned over and hurled into a plastic wastebasket on the floor next to the bed.

At school, I daydreamed about going home to see Mama clean and fresh and smiling, instead of sleeping on her *What Would Atticus Do?* pillow.

Her snores traveled through the air as I gathered the crumpled sheets of tissues dotting the bed. I emptied the wastebasket into the toilet and scrubbed it in the tub. I grew more anxious about not doing enough to help her stop.

In the evenings after work, Uncle Kevin went to The Blue Rooster to pick up a bowl of soup for Mama and a couple of daily specials for the two of us, compliments of LeRoy. He added cheese biscuits and peach cobbler to round out the meals.

Uncle Kevin took the soup into Mama's bedroom and talked with her until she finished. Then, he and I ate in the living room while playing a game of Monopoly. Whoever lost, cleaned the kitchen.

"It's been two weeks," I said, while tapping the thimble token around the corner to land on Indiana Avenue. "How long does detox take?"

"As long as it takes, we'll get through it." He pointed to the game board. "You owe $90.00 rent." I handed him a fifty and two twenties. "Just remember, she's strong, and detox doesn't kill anyone. Let's think positive and look forward to things being right again."

They grew up as close as two siblings could, with hardworking, good parents and few worries.

Uncle Kevin had graduated high school two weeks before their folks went to Macon for a friend's wedding. On the way home, around 10 pm, shortly past the Perry exit on I-75, an oncoming truck swerved to miss hitting a deer and slammed into their car head-on.

With no immediate family to help, they had to depend on each other to get past the shock and sadness.

Because he was eighteen, the community auxiliary fund secured their stay in the family home until Mama graduated high school. After that, nothing could put a stop to the banker foreclosing on the property.

Whenever I go past the Perry exit, I wonder how different things could have been.

Sure as shootin' the poison left Mama's body. As summer faded away and the leaves turned, she worked her butt off at making things right.

Five evenings a week, she traveled by bus to the outskirts of town. Dove Creek Baptist Church hosted a support group with members who'd dealt with similar addictions.

The men and women rallied around her, shared their techniques to brush away the cravings and temptations, and encouraged her to realize working toward a brighter future was more helpful than dwelling on her feelings of remorse.

# 4

My seventeenth birthday was coming in nine days. While walking home from school, the thought of celebrating at The Southern Belly again after the past year of hell, filled me with memories of love and laughter.

Inside the apartment, I heard Elvis Presley singing "Heartbreak Hotel" and grinned, knowing how much Mama loved the eighth of January. Every year our local radio station plays Elvis songs nonstop to commemorate his birthday.

She told me more than once about the time her friend Molly bought tickets for her and her sister to spend the day at Graceland on Elvis' birthday. The package included a tour of the mansion and a concert on the lawn with *The Memphis Boys*.

"It was my lucky day," she'd say. "Her sis caught the flu, and Molly asked if I'd go with her. She begged me. She said I'd be doing her a big favor."

Remembering back to that day caused her face to beam. "A twenty-three-room mansion," she gushed. "Biggest house I've ever been in, Harper, with a jungle room and a trophy room, and a tall wrought-iron gate all around it. And, they buried him in a fancy graveyard called the Meditation Garden."

At the end of the tour, the staff served squares of Elvis' favorite cake, with crushed pineapple and cream cheese frosting on *Happy Birthday* paper plates. Molly ate with the others, but Mama wrapped hers in a napkin to take home and save in the freezer. On January 8th, one year later, she defrosted it and had Elvis cake for breakfast.

I opened the front door with a surge of happiness. *Well, now, if your baby leaves you.* I sang along. *And you got a tale to tell. Just take a walk down Lonely Street...* I caught a whiff of chopped onions and bell peppers cooking on the stove and headed for the kitchen.

Mama was slumped like a tossed-aside rag doll on the floor by the cupboards under the sink. Her U2 Vertigo Tour t-shirt had bunched up around her torso. The outline of her ribs poked through her skin, and her pink underwear had slipped halfway down her hips.

"Mama," I screamed.

She didn't move.

My head pounded. I dropped to the floor to shake her awake. A foam-like goo, thinner than vomit, trickled from her mouth, past her chin, and into her hair. Her eyes were half open. A heat inside me grew too intense to bear.

"Where's the phone?" I shouted. "What the fuck, Mama?"

She usually hung her purse on her bedroom doorknob. I had to leave to get to it, twisting to look back at her the whole time. I released the purse and dug inside for the cell. My heart nearly tore apart when I felt a plastic pill bottle. I snatched it out, saw it was empty, dropped it on the floor, and moaned. "No, Mama, no." My voice sounded like a tire losing air.

Stumbling back to the kitchen, I dialed.

"911, what's your emergency?"

"It's my mama," I said in that small voice, looking at a yellowish bruise on her hip. "She's on the floor."

"Is she breathing?"

"I don't think so. I think she's dead."

"What's your location?"

My brain went empty. "Oh my God," I yelled. "Oh, my God. I can't remember our address."

"That's okay. Do you know what street it is?"

It was all I needed to shake it back into my head. "Send someone, please send someone. Quick."

"Did you perform CPR?"

"No." My voice came back to full volume. "I never learned it. Did you send someone?"

"Tell me exactly what happened?"

"I don't know what happened. There's shit coming out of her mouth," I screamed. "Did you fucking send someone?" I threw the phone against the kitchen wall. It ricocheted back and hit my leg. The dispatcher was still talking, but I hung up and called Uncle Kevin. His phone went straight to message.

"She's dead. I think Mama's dead. It's my fault. Where are you? Oh, God, where are you?"

I knew she would never want the paramedics to see her like that. I gently pulled up her panties and tugged the shirt down to cover them, then ripped a section of paper towel from the roll on the counter and tried to wipe the goop off her face and out of her hair. I turned off the stove and then stayed beside her on the floor. And all the while, Elvis was singing. *Love me tender, love me sweet, never let me go.*

It felt like time had no end before the sirens drowned out the radio. Then the paramedics came in with a gurney and defibrillator, and a crisp white sheet to cover her with.

On that day, Elvis would have been eighty-four years old if he hadn't overdosed. Mama was thirty-eight.

# 5

# Libby

# 1966

On Friday, December 31, the last day of 1965, Libby Carlson stood on the sidewalk and watched an enormous Mayflower moving van pull out of her best friend's driveway.

The Nolan's house had always been Libby's safe place, and Rachael her salvation. Her father had changed jobs. The move would take them cross country, from the Iron Range town of North Forks, Minnesota, to Berkeley, California.

Waving to the back of the truck, Libby couldn't smile, much less breathe without effort.

"Come inside and stop sniveling," her mother yelled out.

Long before that remark, Libby realized her mother would never understand her heartache, despair, and loneliness because the woman had no ability to care about her.

She paced the kitchen running her fingers across the Saint Bernadette pendant around her neck. "I'm sick of seeing you mope around. You have everything to be grateful for."

Libby knew what would come next and, this time, was prepared.

"Grateful," her mother said again. "You know, your brother's dead, and you're not."

"Of course, I know he's dead. Not only was I here when it happened, you constantly tell me."

It felt good to finally say something.

"Don't you be sassing back to me."

Her mother's meanness generally struck when her father wasn't around. Libby knew he knew, and she longed for him to intervene.

Sometimes she reflected on what her mother had been like before Eric's leukemia diagnosis. Had there been happy days, free of worry and anger? Had she found joy in anything?

Libby and Rachael wrote to each other twice a week, languishing over the cruelty of grown-ups and the misery of being so far apart. The letters were a burst of sunshine. They soothed her and reassured her it wasn't Rachael's choice to leave.

She stacked these nuggets of connection in an empty shoebox and re-read them often through that especially harsh winter.

When the snow had melted in late April, and sunshine spread over North Forks, Rachael's letters abruptly stopped. Libby's continued, filled with questions. *What happened? Are you okay? Oh, please let me know what's going on.* Finally, in June, an envelope arrived. Libby's heart soared as she took it to her bedroom.

*Libby,* Rachael wrote. *Absolutely nothing's wrong. Everything's groovy. There's just so much to do here. I've been too busy to write you. My world has expanded. Out here, the sun shines all winter and there's a whole new psychedelic art scene inspired by drugs and trippy visions. I haven't tried magic mushrooms or LSD yet, but my mind's totally blown since I started toking up.*

An entire page detailed her obsession with a new band—The Jefferson Airplane—and how their music changed her life. The lead singer, Marty, invited Rachael to hang with them backstage after their gigs, and she hasn't missed a show since.

She ended the letter with, *I never realized how small North Forks (and maybe the whole mid-west life) is. Small thinking, small ideas, small expectations. I'm having such a blast, but I'm not sure you'd dig it.*

The words chafed Libby's eyes in the way specks of grit would. She was no longer the friend Rachael told secrets to or practiced dancing the cha-cha with. She felt like a heap of soot swept into a corner and left behind. Sadness constantly pulsed through her.

# 6

Each Fourth of July, the Carlson's invited a smattering of select people to their house for a backyard barbeque.

The only reason Libby felt like celebrating that year was the chance to spend time with her Aunt Sandy. She didn't visit often, but when she did, Libby was drawn to her the way a flower seeks the sun. She was the one shining leaf on their wilted family tree.

Aunt Sandy arrived early, wearing a red, white, and blue t-shirt, and carrying a hundred Red Devil firecrackers and two boxes of assorted Astronaut fireworks. She danced around the side of the house to the backyard, whistling *Yankee Doodle Dandy*. Libby ran to greet her and help take the load to the far side of the yard.

Guests laid out salads and side dishes on the picnic table and plates of hotdogs and burgers were set by the grill.

Libby and Sandy had corn duty. They stood together at the kitchen sink, picking corn silk off the cobs and talking about Sandy's plan for the evening's fireworks show.

"Let's take a break," Sandy said as casual as a breeze. "Will you to walk out front with me?"

Libby wiped her hands and followed Sandy down the porch steps leading to the driveway where she had parked her Karman Ghia coup.

"You know how much I love this car?"

"I sure do." Libby stepped forward and swiped her hand over the front fender. "Did you name her Sweet Pea because of her color?"

"The manufacturer calls it lizard-green." Aunt Sandy smiled. "At first, I thought about calling her Split Pea because Lizard didn't seem right. As soon as I drove her off the lot, she was Sweet Pea to me. That was five years ago. And now I have to let her go."

"Let her go?" Libby almost gasped.

"I need a bigger car for my new job, but I don't want her to go to a stranger," Sandy said in a serious tone. "You never know what they might do, so, if you're in the market for a car, I've decided to sell her to you for twenty-five dollars."

Libby's breath caught.

"I'm... really? Twenty-five dollars? She's worth thousands."

Sandy's chin jutted forward. She stood erect, like her brother, Libby's father, often did. Her voice went soft.

"This has nothing to do with the price. It's about love. I'm sure you'll love her as much as I do. And it's about my love for you. Think of Sweet Pea as my Independence Day gift to you." She cleared her throat with a cough. "Listen, Libby, I know your mom is hard on you. If she gives you any guff about this here transaction of ours, you let me know. I'll take care of it."

Having Sweet Pea lessened the burden of losing Rachel, and with long drives through the back roads of the north country, the weight of her loss slowly lightened with each mile.

# 7

Six days after Christmas, Libby stood in the drab living room staring at the same bubble lights on the tree she'd looked at for seventeen years.

As she turned to leave, her heart skipped at the sight of an envelope placed next to the plastic reindeer on the dining table. The exaggerated loops on the front were Rachael's.

In a rush, Libby nicked the tip of her finger as she tore open the back flap and pulled a newspaper page from the envelope. It unfolded easily. A dab of her blood stained the corner.

The bizarre image of a disheveled man with matted hair and an unruly beard filled the page. He stared at her intensely from a large, menacing third eye on his forehead.

*The San Francisco Oracle, Volume 1, No. 5.*

Lacy lettering bordered the page, creating intricate, hard-to-read words arranged in an eerie design.

She studied the writing. *A Gathering of the Tribes for a Human Be-In • Saturday, January 14, 1967, • 1-5 pm • Free • Golden Gate Park.*

The paper named speakers she had never heard of. It said all local San Francisco rock bands would be there. She wondered if Jefferson Airplane was one of them.

*Bring food to share. Bring flowers, beads, costumes, feathers, bells, cymbals, flutes, and flags.*

Next to the man's menacing face, Rachael had written, *"This is where I'll be on your birthday!"*

Puzzled and hopeful, Libby accepted it as a Christmas present and an invitation. Rachael had been gone one year to the day.

"When did this envelope come?" Libby asked her mother.

"A couple of days ago. Maybe a week."

"A week? Why didn't you tell me?"

Her mother shrugged. "I set it on the table, didn't I?" She shook her head and added, "It didn't seem important. Try not to be one of those people, for God's sake."

"Those people? What people?"

"Useless," she said, dismissing herself with a wave.

*Don't be a bore. Stop acting like a victim. You sure are lazy.* Her mother's affronts were nothing new. She'd stiffen or cast her eyes away when Libby got close. The word useless would be the last insult.

On Monday, the day after New Year, she called Jason, the manager of the North Forks Dairy Queen. Libby had started her part-time job stocking supplies and helping with backup duties for the front-end employees. When she became skilled at the signature curly top, Jason promoted her to the customer service window.

Her excuse for not coming to work that afternoon—food poisoning.

"I've had it before. It's nasty," Jason said. "Take all the time you need, and let me know when you feel better."

She drove Sweet Pea to a place she'd never been before. General Jim's Army Navy Surplus Store occupied the better part of a strip mall three towns over from North Forks.

The cavernous building of all things masculine felt strangely seductive. A world unto its own. Libby wandered, scouting out useful items for her top-secret cross-country trip.

The scent of rubber dominated. She marveled at the clutter—the piles and racks. Bins of gas masks, cargo straps, and other accessories of war lined the windowless walls. Lingering for more than an hour, she stroked the toes of combat boots and tapped the tops of helmets. A pair of German WWII binoculars tempted her. *Be practical.*

She took a three-season sleeping bag, a GI-style canteen with a shoulder strap, a military messenger bag, and a Swiss Army Knife to the front counter. $27.97.

With plenty of room to spare in Sweet Pea's bonnet, she returned for some second-thought items. Two bandanas, a jean vest, and a pair of leather sandals cost her another $9.29, leaving $298.00 left from the money hidden in the tin box under the bed.

On the way home, Libby stopped at the three motels in North Forks to ask about their daily rates.

After her parents' room went dark, she sat in bed studying the road map across her lap, looking over the various highways and roads that resembled veins and arteries holding the country together.

The most straightforward route was to get to Iowa, drive west through Nebraska, Wyoming, Utah, Nevada, and straight on to San Francisco. But, her eyes kept wandering to the southern option across Route 66. It looked to be about five hundred miles longer and might mean leaving a day earlier, but the chances of getting stranded in a snowstorm or blizzard on the northern route could slow her down even more.

The T.V. show, *Route 66*, with Tod and Buz traveling the country in their Corvette convertible was one of her favorites, and cinched her choice. She'd drive to its end, in Santa Monica, California, then head north.

Sweet Pea got twenty-one mpg on average. Using the map scale, Libby estimated the trip to be around twenty-seven hundred miles and rounded her calculation to three thousand. If all went well, and the gas war kept the prices between twenty-five to twenty-nine cents a gallon, it would cost about $38.61 to get there.

By the glow of a bedside light, Libby worked for four nights. First, hand-sewing the two bandana's into halter tops and fashioning a headband from leftover black and gold trim. She stitched daisies across the back panel of the denim vest and outlined the petals with large satin stitches. She silently thanked her Home Economics teacher, Mrs. Lerner, for each new petal.

Saturday evening, she waited for her parents to leave at 6:00 pm to play bingo at the church. At 6:15 pm she took her money from the tin box, slid it into an inside zipper of the messenger bag, stuffed the pockets and compartments with her must-haves, and glanced at the diary Aunt Sandy had given her for Christmas. She stuffed it in a front pocket.

Anxiety guided her as she rushed to gather clothes from her drawers and closet and pack them on the small bench that served as Sweet Pea's back seat. Then, the new sleeping bag, some shoes, and her pillow. She'd wear her fur-collared car coat.

The leg from North Forks to Joplin would be the longest of the trip. She planned to be 200 miles from home before her parents' alarm rang in the morning, when her mom's slippers would slide across the kitchen floor and the aroma of coffee percolating on the stove filled the house. Her mother would be hunched over the Formica table reading the paper, with her thin hair wrapped in tight coil pin-curls secured with silver clips. Her father would join her by seven. She'd make him eggs and bacon.

# 8

The crescent moon smiled in the winter sky. Barely breathing for fear of waking one of her parents, Libby opened the car door, released the hand brake, and pushed Sweet Pea down the driveway to the street. Through the early dawn and frigid air, they trudged past the red-brick homes of the Solbergs and the Mitchells to the end of the block.

Once at the stop sign, she slipped into the seat, turned the key, and forced herself to breathe steadily. There was no time or room for second thoughts.

By the onset of dawn's hazy climb, Libby's notion of time transformed from minutes and hours into mile markers and exit signs. Not a single human on the planet knew of her whereabouts. Not even Rachael. An intoxicating freedom grew with each mile.

*Passion. This feeling is the closest thing to passion I've known.*

She freed her ponytail from the band and rolled down her window to let in the frigid Minnesota air. The pungent scent of pine mingled through her hair for what might be the last time.

Her first stop was The Golden Lantern in Saint Cloud, for breakfast. She didn't stop again until the Iowa state line, where she pulled off the road to collect topsoil. With the help of her Swiss Army Knife, she loosened the dirt and scooped up a handful from Minnesota and one from Iowa and dropped it into a paper bag

By the end of the trip, with a short stop at each state line, she'd have an irreplaceable mosaic of clay and sand representing her own blend of freedom.

On the long stretch toward Joplin, Missouri, she silenced the hiss of the radio static and listened to the steady drum of Sweet Pea's engine. Missouri was the furthest from home she'd ever been. There were still twenty-five hundred miles ahead, and her emotions bounced between feeling wonderfully alone, foolishly alone, and plain old foolish.

On the outskirts of Osceola, a billboard announced the fifth anniversary of the Clarke County Hospital. It caused her to remember back to the time Eric died—the child her parents most loved—the perfect one.

He had been five when Libby was born, and he thought no more of her than he did of the lonely goldfish circling the bowl on the credenza, or a discarded pair of shoes.

Her parents doted over him like a fragile treasure. Libby wasn't to enter his room without permission, which rarely came.

"You'll just get in the way," her mother would say. Over time, she'd rather be in her own room nurturing her stuffed animals and wondering how her mother could love Eric so much and not her.

When he died two weeks before her tenth birthday, Libby foolishly believed it was finally her time to shine in her parents' eyes, but their devotion to him only grew stronger. Her mother served on the Childhood Leukemia Foundation and the Faith Lutheran Church boards. Her father volunteered on the Northern Plains Dare to Dream project. Their grief over Eric continued nightly at the dinner table, with story after story of the boy who could do no wrong.

It took close to fourteen hours and three stops for gas to reach the outskirts of Joplin. She had driven through lunch, and the hollow in her stomach moaned for food. Libby pulled off the highway and drove into the parking lot of a Thriftway market.

The floor of the deli aisle felt tacky under her shoes, like it didn't want her to rush past. A sign on the cheese and cold cuts display read *Deal of the Day—Oscar Mayer Variety Pack 97¢*.

Along with the cold cuts, she took a box of Saltines, a jar of Skippy, two bananas, and a pack of plastic utensils to the checkout counter.

Back inside Sweet Pea, she built two peanut butter and banana on saltine sandwiches. While eating, she focused on a neon sign across the highway flashing, *Falls Motel, Vacancy, $6.00.* Her head settled back against the seat, and the day slipped away.

A man rapped on the passenger window. "You okay?" He stared inside. "You okay?" he asked again.

Her pulse shot up. "Yes, yes. I'm fine," she yelled. "I just fell asleep. I'm fine."

The Falls Motel sign flashed and flashed.


No longer hungry, she sat on the floral bedspread and organized her receipts for the day— $18.05, leaving her $279.95.

She flopped back on the bed and looked up. Fragments of her rushed plan began to descend from the popcorn ceiling in specks of doubt and the fear that her newfound confidence was a fraud. Tears seeped from her eyes. *I cannot be afraid of being afraid.*

Unable to stop her mind, she stepped outside into the cold air. The whine of the highway turned to white noise as she paced up and down the walkway to the reception office several times before going inside.

When checking in, she hadn't noticed the worn sofa and two orange vinyl chairs by the bay window facing the pool area. The man who helped her an hour earlier was gone. A sign next to a bell on the counter said, *Ring Once For Service.*

A black pay phone was mounted on the wall near the front desk. *Had her parents called the police? Did they know she was gone? Did they care?*

The receiver felt solid between her shoulder and chin. She pulled a dime from her pocket and dropped it in the coin slot, knowing the call wouldn't go well.

Three rings. Her mother answered.

She fought back the impulse to slam the receiver back onto its cradle.

"It's Libby," she said with a quiver.

A silence followed. Libby leaned her shoulder against the wall and focused on the rack of tourism brochures, Grand Falls, Northpark Mall, Bonnie and Clyde's Joplin Hideout.

After a small eternity, her mother's voice glided slowly into her ear. "Yes, Libby. What do you want?"

"I wanted to let you know I'm okay." She pictured her mother's pinched brow.

"Shame on you, Libby Carlson." There was no sign of worry in her voice.

"I'm going to California to see Rachael."

"You waited until now to tell us? Your brother wouldn't have done something like this."

"Yes, I know he wouldn't have. But, as you like to say, he's dead, and I'm not."

"If this is what you want, fine."

Libby whispered, "I'll let you go," before the line went dead.

Close to eighteen years of her parents' lack of concern amplified the meaning of those words, *I'll let you go.* She returned the receiver to the cradle and sat on the sofa by the bay window.

Her second grade teacher, Mrs. Hannigan, came to mind. Each morning when Libby went into class, Mrs. Hannigan had written on the chalkboard, *A Sentence A Day, In The Most Positive Way*, and then she wrote an optimistic message underneath.

Together, the class would recite the sentence three times before it vanished under the swipe of the eraser. Libby looked forward to the daily dose of magic words. They helped with her sadness.

Each footstep up the walkway back to the room felt immense, like her shoes were made of cement. The chilly air hit the wet streaks on her cheeks and caused more to fall. Once back in the room, she reached for the diary.

> January 8, 1967—Sunday
> *Made it to Joplin. Called home. It was nothing new. I'm not sure what I'm doing. I can't go back. I will probably never be in North Forks again. I know that things will be better when I see Rachael. I'll live with the Nolans until I figure out my life. Oh, please let things get better.*

Sleep came fast.

Standing in a field of mustard grass, she saw Eric dangling from a tarnished chandelier dressed in a threadbare hospital gown. The chandelier lurched toward her and hovered above her head.

Armed with a fly swatter, she slashed at his legs over and over. Every time she stopped swatting, the chandelier lights flickered and Eric's legs grew longer.

# 9

Libby and Sweet Pea left Joplin and drove toward the western horizon on the paved highway called the Mother Road—Route 66. They would cross three time zones and six state lines in three days before reaching the Pacific Ocean. Sweet Pea required a leisurely pace, and the January weather assured light traffic.

At the Kansas border, she gathered her dirt and set the bag on the passenger seat. After a short thirteen-mile slice of the state, she collected more at the Oklahoma border.

The long stretches between the populated towns offered views of yellow-green hills and rust-colored boulders. With no radio reception came a boredom she hadn't expected. Libby thought the solitude of the road would give her space to sort out her past and dream of the future, but a sense of doom had tunneled into her mood.

In the Texas panhandle, passing Palo Duro Canyon, the geography changed drastically from the

Midwest to the Southwest with a dusting of snow-
topped red rocks and cacti. Lazy shadows from the
winter clouds glided across the land, and time
lingered.

At the end of that second day, under a sky
bursting with a billion stars, they had made it to
Glenrio in New Mexico. Low on Saltines, she stopped
at a small cement block cafe and gas station called
the Little Juarez Diner, for her first restaurant meal
since St. Cloud.

There were no customers inside, only a dark-
skinned woman on the last stool next to the wall. She
sliced limes and onions on a wooden board. A pink
ribbon secured her long black hair at the nape of her
neck.

Libby had seen Mexicans in movies before, like
Dolores del Rio and Ricardo Montalban, but she had
never seen one in person.

Five stools separated them. She watched the
woman's practiced hands tend to her work. The
building's warmth and the aromas of unfamiliar
spices soothed her. A handwritten menu hung on the
wall.

A man wearing a worn apron set a silverware
and a paper placemat in front of her.

"Bueno's tardes."

Libby twisted her mouth, embarrassed. "Do you
speak English?"

"Si, si, Seniorita. I speak."

"I've never had Mexican food before and can't read the menu."

"No hay problema." The man looked amused. "The gringos, they always order the beef taco with beans and rice." He pointed to the menu. "El taco de carne con arroz y frijoles is what you want."

"Thank you."

Twelve hundred miles from North Forks, she had transported herself to another land. She thought back to her mother's reaction when she called from Joplin. As horrible as it had been, it brought satisfaction, the way viewing a body at a funeral brings closure to the mourners.

At the Little Juarez Diner in Glenrio, New Mexico, she began to accept her life was now truly in her own hands.

"Muy caliente. Hot plate," the man said as he delivered the meal. To the right of the large dish, chunks of soft cheese topped a base of creamy refried beans. A heap of red-orange rice filled the other side. The taco rested on its side. Salsa and shredded lettuce fell from the shell.

Not sure how to eat the taco, she looked at the senora and shrugged. The woman mimed picking up an invisible taco and biting into the air between her hands.

"Thank you."

"De nada."

The food burst with intoxicating flavors she'd never tasted before. Without realizing, she gobbled up the plan to eat half for dinner and package the rest for the next day.

As the man cleared her plate and collected her money, she said, "Excuse me, sir, is there a place to spend the night near here?"

"Si, Seniorita. The Longhorn." He pointed out the window.

"Thanks," she said. "Do you know what they charge? Is it expensive?"

"Si, es muy expensive. Seniorita, I tell you what, if you fill your car with gas from my pumps and not theirs, you can park behind the cafe overnight for free. We live in our camper out back. Is safe."

His wife nodded reassuringly.

She gave them a small hand wave. "I'm Libby."

"Me, I'm Javier. Mi esposa es Soledad."


Libby woke before dawn, determined to stay in a room with a bed and heater the next night.

She used the small restroom behind the cafe to clean up, and took extra paper towels to wipe the moisture and dead insects from Sweet Pea's windows.

When she turned the key to start the engine and switch on the heater, the dashboard gauges bounced and the lights flickered.

"Come on, Sweet Pea, you can do this."

Again, the car wouldn't respond when she turned the key. Her heart raced at the thought of being stuck in Glenrio for days because of the stupid choice not to get a check-up before the long drive.

Libby wallowed in doom for an hour before Javier and his wife opened the door to their camper. Soledad waved as she walked to the cafe. Javier came toward Libby.

She rushed to him. "Javier, my car is dead. Can you help me?"

"Muerto? Por que? Why?"

"I don't know. But it won't start, and I have to leave."

He reached in the car to try the ignition for himself, with the same result, then confidently strode toward the front to look under the hood.

"No, Javier, the engine's in the back."

He laughed. "Like the loco beetle bugs."

Libby stood by his side as he crouched to study Sweet Pea's backside. He pointed to a greenish-white growth covering the battery terminals.

"Corrosion de la bateria," he said and smiled. No problemo. Volvere en un minuto. Stay here. One minute."

Libby waited anxiously, unable to take her eyes away from the alien growth eating each end of the battery.

Javier returned with a bucket of baking soda and water in one hand, and two brushes in the other—one with sturdy wires for the overall cleaning and a toothbrush for the smaller areas.

He poured a small amount of water over the battery, demonstrated how to scrub it, and said, "I go prepare for the Desayuno." He left her to solve the problem.

Javier and Soledad sent her on her way with a clean battery and a rice and bean burrito.

"You are my lucky star, Javier."

Heading west through New Mexico, winds and fluttering snowflakes amplified the region's winter purples and pinks. One after another, the curio shops along the road tempted her to stop. The life-size murals of native people painted on the walls of The Old Crater Trading Post did the trick.

The Old Crater specialized in all things Navajo, including jewelry, rugs, and alabaster sculptures. The sprawling stucco hall was as fascinating as General Jim's Surplus had been.

In a glass bowl by the cash register, colorful Zuni beaded dolls, smaller than a matchbox, called out to Libby. She picked up each one. The figure with the yellow and black headdress felt best in the palm of her hand. She named it Christopher and hung it on Sweet Pea's rearview mirror.

An hour and a half into Arizona, Libby turned off the highway in Holbrook and drove through the main drag for more groceries.

While stopped at a red light she noticed a cluster of white concrete teepees half a block up the street.

The WigWam Motel. The sign out front asked, "Have you slept in a Wigwam lately?"

After checking in, she parked in front of her assigned teepee. Inside, the walls angled up to a peak ten feet high, where a light bulb dangled from a thick electrical wire.

She placed her bag on the colorful Serape blanket used as the bedspread. Warm, exhausted, and feeling safe, she went to bed, intending to get an early start, to Santa Monica during daylight.

Before falling asleep, memories of her summers in Minnesota came back. The first week in June, Rachael's father climbed a ladder to the garage rafters and brought down his WW II yellow inflatable life raft for the girls to use as a wading pool. He put it on the grass in their backyard and fiddled with a valve. Abracadabra, the raft inflated. The girls spent their happiest hours splashing together in the middle of the backyard.

*Rachael will be so happy to see me. Our reunion is all the love I need.*

Through the night, the showerhead continually dripped on the metal floor pan until it was overtaken by the thunder of freight trains barreling down the tracks next to the Wigwams. She woke at 1 am, 2 am, then 3 am. At 3:30 am, she left.

At two in the afternoon, she had reached land's end. Libby stood in a mist of salty air at the intersection of Pier Avenue and Ocean Park.

Across the street, on the Santa Monica Pier, a futuristic, space-age amusement park hovered over an angry ocean of churning whitecaps. Seagulls squawked and circled above the awe-inspiring sight called Pacific Ocean Park.

She thanked the noisy shower and the freight trains for her early exit, which made it possible to spend the rest of the day in Santa Monica and still get to Rachael's the next evening.

The waves lapped against the shore as she navigated over the uneven planks to the small ticket booth. An old man took a dollar, two dimes, and five pennies in exchange for an all-access ticket to the rides and exhibits.

Beyond the entrance, the Neptune's Kingdom walkway led her past dioramas replicating the Roman God Of The Sea's lair into the heart of the park. Beach Boys' music blasted, and lights flashed. Spinning rides, futuristic structures, and the cartoon atmosphere replenished her with childish wonder.

She passed up the Sea Serpent Roller Coaster. The motion sickness incident at the Minnesota State Fair was still too fresh. Instead, she sat in the bleachers of a show called the Sea Circus.

Porpoises, dolphins, and two seals named Dinky and Rob Roy leaped and twirled across a pool under an open-air big top. Their beauty and athleticism took her breath and brought her pure joy.

At 5 pm, on that chilly January day, Libby climbed aboard Ocean Skyway gondola and rode alone in the round bubble suspended 75 feet above the pier. It bobbled and swayed, dangling over the ocean a half-mile beyond the park. Her mother's voice entered her head. *Your brother wouldn't have done something like this.*

Libby looked to the horizon, overwhelmed and amazed at how big the world was. In the last one or two seconds before the sea swallowed the sun, she witnessed the brief green flash.

The gondola returned to the pier and loitered over the clatter of the tourists below. Like a freed bird soaring above it all, she once again reveled in the glorious yet terrifying pleasure that no one could imagine her being there.

Before walking back into reality, Libby stopped at Fisherman Cove souvenir shop and bought a decal for Sweet Pea.

# 10

# Harper

# 2019

After Mama died, Uncle Kevin took me to his place, where together we began the first chapter of grief.

Just like he did with Mama after their folks died, he served as my rock during those days of confusion and all-consuming sorrow. And, on the worst day of all, he held my hand while our best shoes crunched over the gravel path to the cemetery plot, where they set her in the ground next to her folks.

He lived on the outskirts of town where the road meandered under moss-dripped trees, past the long stretch of wild hydrangea shrubs.

The house had areas with chipped paint, and the porch sloped, but the inside was a place of warmth and love. My whole life, the three of us gathered there to celebrate most holidays, holding on to some of the old family traditions passed down from their folks and adding a couple of new ones, like BBQ wings for Easter and Moon Pies instead of Pumpkin Pies for Thanksgiving.

A week after the funeral, he drove me through the familiar streets of town back to the apartment. I couldn't understand how everyone still went about their business, like nothing had changed.

When he pulled his truck up to the building we'd lived in for so long, the gardening crew still raked the leaves and mowed the lawn, like always. I wondered if they even knew she died.

With a box of 30-gallon Hefty bags under his arm, Uncle Kevin led the way up the stairs to the platform by the door. Inside, cold, heartless air had chased away the warmth we knew. I couldn't bring myself to look inside the kitchen and rushed past the overstuffed loveseat straight to my room.

Crumpled shirts and dirty jeans covered the floor of my closet. I yanked the clean clothes off the wire hangers and watched them swing like spastic teeter-totters.

When I couldn't find the mate to a pink sock, my heart ached. It seemed best to move on from the closet and come back later.

Under my bed, I found the plastic sword Uncle Kevin had given me years before. I remembered opening the front door to see a handsome knight in a gold cape holding a sword. He bowed and said, "May

I have the honor of escorting you to your first movie, my princess?"

I curtsied and jumped with excitement. "What movie?"

"It's called *Enchanted*, and it's about a beautiful red-headed princess like you."

My throne was red, with a cup holder. I wore a tiara and held my own box of popcorn. My knight wrapped his hand around mine whenever the evil queen of Andalasia came on screen.

I set the sword on top of the bed to take with me. Next, I peeled the scotch tape off the four corners of my Billie Eilish and Lady Gaga posters. Lady Gaga covered a crack in the wall that looked like a jagged pitchfork. It begged me to run my finger over it one last time.

The Commemorative Quarters I'd collected and stored in my Walker's shortbread tin rattled when I brought it out of the dresser drawer. For all the times I had dropped a new coin inside the tin, I still didn't have Delaware, Oregon, and Hawaii.

I could hear Uncle Kevin cleaning out Mama's room, and wondered what the point of collecting things was, if you're just going to die.

My legs went weak when I lifted the mason jar from the windowsill—the one brimming with random bird feathers I'd found over the years. I sat on the bed.

When Uncle Kevin heard my sobs, he came into the room and sat beside me.

"You know when Scout's talking about Dell?" I said.

He rubbed my back. "I know you're talkin' about the book, but I'm not as up on it as you and Ellie."

"The part when Scout says, 'With him, life was routine; without him, life was unbearable.' I'm feeling a lot like that right now. Can we go and come back tomorrow?"

Melancholy was still with me the following morning. I lingered in bed, having a hard time getting clear-headed.

"Stay here, Harper. Stay in bed," Uncle Kevin insisted before he left.

Every part of me knew he shouldn't have gone alone. His heart was as heavy as mine, and it didn't take more than an hour before my selfishness turned plain old ugly. The longer I languished in the house, the more I struggled with the shame of what Mama might be thinking.

By noon, I texted Megan. She was in Tifton with her mom and couldn't take me to the apartment. I could walk the twelve miles but wouldn't get there until four o'clock.

To salvage my worth, I gathered potatoes and onions from the steel bin, carrots and turnips from the crisper, and a chuck roast from the freezer to put together an apology meal.

Uncle Kevin hardly noticed the comforting smell from the oven when he came through the back door holding Mama's *What Would Atticus Do?* pillow and a shoe box without a lid. His face broadcast a day of sadness and exhaustion. With dust in his eyebrows and sweat stains on his shirt, he emptied the things in his arms onto the kitchen table and settled into a chair.

"These are for you."

Mama's comb and brush were on top of the things in the shoe box. I brought the brush to my face, smelled her thin brown strands nestled in the bristles, and set it back down with the hairclips and ribbons she used to tie her hair back.

Next to the box, he had set Mama's crystal pendent necklace and her ring with the tiny garnet— my birthstone.

My intention was to concentrate only on Uncle Kevin when he got home. Still, the sight of her things caused a deep cramp inside my ribs, and I dropped the kitchen towel I'd been wiping my hands on. As I bent to pick it up, water collected in my eyes. The towel served as my blotter.

He rapped the table. "I'll shower, and then we can have some of that good-smelling meal you've been working on. Emptying the truck can wait 'til morning."

# 11

A long, skinny driveway meandered past the side of Uncle Kevin's house to a back lot where a broken-down garage watched over the sprawling oak tree I had nicknamed Charlotte.

A canvas tarp covered an old Honda Civic permanently perched on cement blocks under the attached carport.

In his spare time, he cleaned up damaged military foot lockers collected from yard sales. Then he stored them in his garage, all 23 of them, along with busted tools and buckets of rusty nails. Determined to turn the garage into a proper place for me to live, he listed all the lockers on eBay and Craigslist, and threw out the busted tools.

If you wanted your mail delivered on time, Uncle Kevin was your man. But when it came to roofing, plumbing, or electrical, he needed help and knew it. After I moved in with him, his construction buddies came over every weekend for beer and pizza delivery. Along with their ladders and power tools, they brought loud music and laughter, and they transformed the neglected garage into a safe, private place for me to live.

Halfway through the remodel, he bought a long wood-framed window from a bankruptcy auction, and insisted on installing it himself. With guidance from his buddy's, he measured twice, cut out the studs, sawed through the wall and installed the window for an unobstructed view of Charlotte.

"Oh, that's nice, Uncle Kevin. Real nice," I said, with pure admiration.

"I figure this way you can keep watch over her as she changes through the seasons."

I'd spent hours beneath her dangling moss, and climbed over her stretched-out branches that spread more sideways than upward.

After the window went in, Uncle Kevin's plumber friend Dooky installed a cast iron sink below it. By May, the drywall went up and it was easy to see the old garage would soon be a cozy place with a hand-built ladder going up to the bedroom loft.

The last weekend before the final coat of paint when on, Dooky brought his brother along. Dressed in a mechanic's jumpsuit, the man sprang from the truck's passenger side and went toward the back. He looked like a super-sized version of Dooky. He released the tailgate, pulled out a floor jack and a big toolbox, and transported everything to the carport in one trip.

I hurried to the back stoop and watched the giant man whip the tarp off the Honda with the flair of a matador, and spread it on the ground.

It might have been foolish of me to imagine anyone could bring it back to life. Just the same, I felt the lightness of hope.

"Hi," I said to Dooky's brother, watching his beefy hands wrap around the tools and lay them on the tarp. "Is it fixable?"

He opened the hood. "Offhand, I'd say I'm not sure. Depends on how much damage the critters have done. They like to chew on the hoses and such." He waved a finger over the engine when he talked. "It's like playing a game of roulette. I'll switch those out and put in fresh fluids. Of course it'll need a new battery. I've got one in the truck we can use. Then we'll spin the wheel and hope we don't land on double zeros."

"Where do you think the term Russian Roulette came from?"

Don't know."

"What does Roulette mean, anyway?"

"Beat's me."

I spit question after question at the man until he lumbered over to me, stood to his full height, and said, "Miss Harper, I need you to step back and stop asking questions."

"Oh, okay. Sure." I went out back to sit under Charlotte.

By dusk on Sunday, that Honda had a fully running engine and a new set of used tires. Dooky's brother turned out to be part mechanic and part magician. He said, "It looks like this leftover got a new beginning, and you'll be driving it down the road toward the Tifton DMV."

I raised my arms to the sky and danced in circles when Uncle Kevin handed me the old Honda key dangling from a leather Ferrari key ring.

"She's all yours," he said. "Take her for a spin."

# 12

On the dry, clear morning of May 24th, Megan and I stood next to each other dressed in identical caps and gowns, along with the other 73 kids on the platform. And yet, without Mama there clutching her hands to her heart and smiling with pride, the day lacked luster.

My life had taken a pause while most of the other kids waiting to receive their diplomas had plans for their futures. I glanced at the cloudless sky for a sign but only saw emptiness.

The sun behind us had been up for hours by the time we assembled on stage. I searched the bleachers, and my mood picked up when I spotted Uncle Kevin beside Megan's mama and LeRoy beside her. All three looked in high spirits.

Principal Calhoun made his way to the podium. In a booming TV announcer voice, he said, "Good morning to all who are here, and welcome to the graduation ceremonies of the class of 2019."

After thanking most of the staff, the Mayor, and the School Superintendent who had come, he said, "I am pleased to call our Class Valedictorian, Thomas Newsome, to come forward and speak to us."

Our cheers echoed through the field.

After they shook hands, Tommy took to the microphone. Holding a book, he looked out to the crowd. Even though I was behind him, I pictured his big grin punctuated by two bottomless dimples.

Tommy said, "My first official duty as a high school graduate will be one of plagiarism." Scattered laughs bounced through the audience. "I'm not the first to give this speech. And because it comes from a genius, I certainly won't be the last. I'm excited to recite the work of the late, the great Dr. Theodor Seuss Geisel." He opened the book. *Oh, The Places You'll Go.*

I hadn't heard those words in years. His wacky idea for a commencement speech ignited a surge of memories of Mama and me sitting together, her reading and me turning the pages. I took hold of Megan's hand. She embraced it and returned a squeeze as tender as a hug.

My heart danced along with the rhyming phrases Tommy recited. I remembered Mama's voice had bounced out those exact words like they were playthings. *The mail, the rain. Yes, or No, or hair to grow.* She took so much pleasure in the fantastical terms. *Enemies prowl. Hakken-Kraks howl. A creek. A leak.* I would breathe in the almond-cherry scent of her Jergen's lotion and watch her finger slide under the sentences.

As his voice swelled toward the finale, my heartbeat sped. The tassel on my cap began to swing, and instead of Tommy's, I heard Mama's voice.

She'd recite her variation of the last verse with an exaggerated southern drawl. Low and soft, she'd murmur, *or Harper Van Warner, my perfect Parfait,* then kiss my nose.

After they called all our names and Principal Calhoun handed out the rolled-up diplomas, the sight of our hats tossed in the air, like a flock of blackbirds with golden tassel tales, will be forever etched in my mind.

And thanks to Tommy Newsome, I spent my graduation ceremony with Mama.

# 13

One morning while in Denny's pouring syrup in each hollow of my pecan waffle, a guy wearing a denim jacket and cowboy boots came through the double doors.

He strolled toward my four-person booth like someone in a slow-motion scene from an old Western. His dark hair fell over his forehead, and he spread his fingers to comb it back, then sat in the space across from me.

He pulled the AirPods from his ears and set them on the table. His steely eyes studied me, and the sides of his mouth turned up. "I heard it said that once in his life, a man must fall in love with a redhead."

I knew Lucille Ball was famous for the quote. Even so, my chest warmed, and then the heat spread over my neck and face. I willed the courage to look at him instead of my waffle, but couldn't think of anything cool to say.

"I'm Edison Le Blanc."

"Harper," I choked out.

"But you can call me Eddie."

"Eddie," I said, testing how it felt in my mouth.

"I also heard redheads are trouble. Is that true?"

"What do you mean, trouble?"

Before he answered, the waitress appeared with her well-practiced smile and an order pad ready.

"Do you mind if I stay?"

My shoulders bounced. "No."

"In that case," he said to the waitress, "I'll have the Lumberjack Slam and a Sprite."

I don't know why he sat at my table or why we started going out, other than the universe can be a real bastard sometimes.


We'd only known each other for two weeks before he brought an extra pair of jeans and his toothbrush to my place. Each time he came by, he left something else behind.

Uncle Kevin had a solid hissy fit. He couldn't say anything nice about Eddie. Nothing. In little more time than it took Eddie to get real comfortable "freeloading," as Uncle Kevin would say, he turned stubborn and headstrong and preferred to spend most of his time and attention playing video games and watching sports.

He ate handfuls of mini Snickers, tossed the wrappers on the floor, and left his used-up mint-flavored dental floss on the sink counter.

Instead of his "beautiful redheaded girl," he called me Harp because he said I always harped at him.

I hadn't worked up the nerve to end it due to the hope that one day he'd give a damn. But mostly, I hadn't ended it because I liked people knowing I had a boyfriend, and I could pretend he loved me.

On Saturday, June 15, I arrived at work five minutes early, marched down the hand tools aisle to the lunch room, and stashed my purse in my storage locker. While putting on my Hickory Springs Hardware Store apron, Vernon, the manager, swung the door open so hard it slammed against the wall, and he walked inside.

One month earlier, he had done the same thing. That time I was eating a piece of honey cake on my afternoon break, and he sat on the bench next to me.

Tender bumps with pus at the tips covered his forehead, and the stink of paint thinner clung to his clothes. I offered him a piece of cake. He shook his head, straightened his back, and smiled like someone was about to take his picture.

He said, "Harper, I'd be grateful if you'd have dinner with me this weekend."

The words buzzed in my ears before settling in. It sounded like something an old man would say. *I'd be grateful.*

After a long silence, I cleared my throat and said, "Well, Vernon, I'm flattered, really I am, but," I looked at his chin rather than his forehead. "I don't mix work with pleasure. It's my policy." It sounded every bit as old-persony as his question had. *Policy?*

Vernon's head jutted forward. He nodded again and again like he'd turned into a bobblehead. His mouth puckered while his head continued to nod.

He said, "I understand," then popped up from the bench and walked out. After he left, the honey cake tasted sour.

Seeing him the second time altered my disposition from good-natured to dreadful. "Morning, Vernon," I said, noticing the manila envelope in his hand.

His skinny finger pointed to the bench in front of the picnic table where we were the last time. "Have a seat, Harper."

He swung his leg over the bench across from me and placed the envelope next to the plastic basket with fast-food ketchup and mustard packs inside. Someone had stamped CONFIDENTIAL on the front.

"Harper?"

"Yeah," I said, hoping he wouldn't ask me out again.

"I'm going to have to let you go."

"What? What the fuck?"

He slid the envelope in front of me. It slammed into my arm.

"Are you kidding? What's this about?" I wrapped my arms tight around me. "Is this because I wouldn't go out with you?"

His eyes were fixed on me, steady and piercing. "Of course not. You sure think a lot of yourself, don't you?"

"No."

"We're scaling back on the weekend shifts." He cracked a smile. "It's our new policy. You know about policies."

I stared into my lap, not moving until he left the room. When the door closed, the place turned silent. My anger had nowhere to go.

The CONFIDENTIAL envelope taunted me. I tore it open so hard one of the papers inside ripped in half. The pink one. Notice of Termination.

*A pink slip, and it's actually fucking pink.*

Still wearing my apron, I drove home to bury myself under the bed covers and suffer my humiliation alone. Three tiny raindrops hit the windshield. I didn't turn the wipers on. By the time I drove to the end of the block, a solid sheet of rain distorted my vision.

Eddie's car was still parked out front when I pulled into the driveway. I slammed the wheel with my hands, and tears joined the raindrops in blurring my life.

He looked right at home watching a Harlem Globetrotters game from my corduroy recliner. Surprised by the intrusion, he shot up from the chair wearing nothing but a pinched face and his white Fruit Of The Looms. He hiked his hands on his hips.

"What're you doing home?" He shook his hair out of his eyes. "Really, what're you doing here?"

The word *home* sounded distorted. My anger found a target.

"Are you talking about my fucking home?" My voice rose, and I screamed, "My Goddamn home? My chair?" I pointed to the chair. "My fucking TV?" I looked at the screen. A Globetrotter was standing on the rim of the hoop, shaking his butt at the camera.

"Get out," I screeched.

"Whoa, what's going on?"

I wiped the dampness from my eyes with the heel of my hands. "I got canned. Do you give a shit?"

He hissed a sarcastic laugh."Not really."

"Get your crap out of here right now, and leave."

He didn't move.

I threw my purse at him. It grazed his arm and tumbled across the floor. Two quarters rolled under the loveseat.

He remained standing.

I cocked my thumb toward Uncle Kevin's house. "I'll get him if I have to."

Eddie picked his jeans off the floor, pulled them on, then darted back and forth, grunting as he shoved his clothes and extras into a flimsy-handled brown bag.

With the bag in one hand and his prized vintage Game Boy in the other, he kicked the screen door open.

"Adios, Harper," he yelled, then turned back to face the door. "That means good riddance in Spanish."

I watched the back of his car spit dark puffs of smoke and heard one piercing backfire as he drove off.

# 14

# Libby

# 1967

Cradled by the tranquil grey ocean to her left and lush sloping hills stippled with cliffside bungalows to her right, the final leg up Highway 101 felt like driving through a painting. She wondered if this much happiness was allowed.

The gas gauge hit empty just before Watsonville. When Libby asked how long it would take to get to Berkeley, the gas station attendant said, "Two hours, give or take."

As she watched his squeegee glide over Sweet Pea's windshield, the questions she hadn't allowed herself to ask materialized. *"What if they have moved? Or have company? What if they took a last-minute trip? What if someone's sick?"*

She took the slip of paper with Rachael's address

and phone number from the glove box and went into the phone booth by the office. No one answered at the Nolan's.

Libby made it to Berkeley proper through the heart-pounding San Francisco traffic and some risky lane changes. She took the first exit to search for a gas station and get directions to Rachael's.

As daylight surrendered to dusk, she turned onto Sacramento Street. Parked under a leafless sycamore on the opposite side of the street from the Nolan's address, she squinted through a shadowy mist at the brown-shingled house. With no car in the drive and the front windows dark, it didn't look like anyone was home.

Watching a streak of pink escape the clouds as the sun set, she reflected on her momentous escape and the chance for a better future while living with the Nolans.

The Zuni doll hung still from the rearview mirror where Libby studied her face, noting the dark circles under her eyes, then she slipped her Keds off and leaned back.

The aroma of freedom coming off the California coastline and her new sense of self, filled her. Every decision made had been hers alone.

A flash of light glistened through the curtains in the Nolan's front windows, and the large glass lantern above the front door washed the steps with light.

The damp air nipped at her skin as she rushed across the asphalt and up the porch. She closed her eyes and searched her mind for just the right affirmation. *There will never be a better moment than this.* She rang the bell.

Rachael's voice yelled out, "Mom, they're here. I'll be back when I'm back."

The front door opened.

Behind the screen, Rachael froze, then she squinted.

"Libby?"

The huge smile Libby had dreamed of was nowhere.

"What are you doing here?"

Rachael's dark, curly hair had turned straight and platinum blond, parted in the middle. It hung past her shoulders. Dark mascara ringed her eyes. The screen remained closed.

"What am I doing here?" Libby threw her arms in the air. "You asked me to come. Oh my God, I'm so happy to see you. I'm finally here after five days and close to three thousand miles."

"Who is it, Rachael?" Libby recognized Mrs. Nolan's voice.

"Um, Libby," Rachael said.

"Libby?"

Wearing a pink velvet bathrobe and a towel turban twisted over her hair, Mrs. Nolan poked her ample body past her daughter and flung the screen open.

"Libby," she yelped. "Libby, Libby, come inside. You'll catch your death." She grabbed Libby's hand and guided her past Rachael into the living room, then embraced her tight. She smelled like a lavender cloud.

Rachael said, "I don't understand. What are you doing here? When did I ever ask you to come? And why didn't you let me know?"

"You sent me the invitation."

"What?"

"For my birthday."

"Invitation? What are you talking about?"

"The page from the Oracle. The Be-In. My birthday."

Rachael frowned. "You kept writing your sad, poor me letters, so I thought you'd like to know I would actually be doing something fun on your birthday. It wasn't an invitation."

"What's going on?"

A black Volkswagen honked from the street and pulled into the driveway, puttering similar to Sweet Pea's sound.

"Sorry, gotta go," Rachael said.

"Wait a minute, young lady," Mrs. Nolan yelled as her daughter darted out the front door. "It's Libby. STOP."

Rachael turned back and shrugged. "You can't show up out of the blue. If you'd called, you would've known I have plans."

Libby's breath stopped as Rachael turned and ran to the waiting car.

Before getting in, Rachael added, "Let me know where you're staying. Maybe we can reminisce sometime."

Afraid she might vomit, she leaned against Mrs. Nolan while the Volkswagen drove off.

Mrs. Nolan coaxed her into the kitchen.

"Sit here."

She pulled a chair from the round oak table. The same table Libby sat at in their old kitchen, in their old town, with the same four green placemats protecting the surface.

The air turned heavy with silence until Mrs. Nolan said, "I'll make you something to eat."

"I'm not hungry."

"Have you eaten today?"

"I don't know."

"You have to eat."

Looking distressed, Mrs. Nolan tightened the belt on her robe and moved toward the stove. Frank Sinatra's easy voice drifted in from another room. "As Time Goes By."

Mrs. Nolan set a grilled cheese sandwich and a bowl of cream of tomato soup in front of Libby. She looked at the woman, her "thank you" barely audible.

Mrs. Nolan patted her towel turban and slumped in the chair across from Libby. "Rachael never mentioned you were coming."

"I wanted it to be a surprise."

"I know it's no consolation, but I'm super happy to see you."

Libby had never noticed the red veins across Mrs. Nolan's cheeks mingled with a patch of blotchy brown spots.

"Tomorrow's my birthday. I thought she was my best friend." Her voice cracked with pain. *This is what it feels like to be stabbed in the back.*

"Oh, Libby dear." Mrs. Nolan closed her eyes. "What just happened breaks my heart." The sadness in her brown eyes mirrored Libby's own misery.

"Did you tell me how you got here?"

"I drove."

"Alone? Do you know how dangerous that is? Do your parents know?"

Libby shrugged and brought a spoonful of soup to her lips. The taste brought back memories of all the times Mrs. Nolan served up a bowl of love for her and Rachael. The thought lingered as the warmth hit her chest.

The North Forks Mrs. Nolan had been the personification of the stoic Midwest mother, always showing patience and endurance. When not reading *Movie Star News* from cover to cover, she spent a good part of her day in the kitchen, in a colorful handmade apron with a scalloped hem, transforming basic ingredients into staples like freshly made mayonnaise and ranch dressing.

Mrs. Nolan rubbed her hand across the highly waxed table. "This move out here was a mistake." Her eyes focused on the wood grain.

Libby's back stiffened. "Mrs. Nolan, are you okay? It doesn't seem like you're okay?"

"No, I'm not okay." Her voice was quiet, and she looked worn out. "Seeing you has brought my emotions to the surface."

"I don't understand."

"I shouldn't be saying this, but I'm terribly unhappy here. This house is too big, the weather is too nice, and the town is too sophisticated."

Her words disoriented Libby. Where was the woman with three first-place blue ribbons from the Itasca County Fair? Two for her double-crust rhubarb pie entries, and one for her Swedish Cardamom Bread made with Red Star Yeast.

"But most of all," Mrs. Nolan added, interrupting Libby's thoughts, "I hate what the move has done to Rachael." She brushed away a tear. "Living here has turned her into someone I don't recognize. Someone mean and ungrateful. She sasses back at everything. Bill thinks it's elevated estrogen levels and normal teen angst, but he's never here."

Her hands cupped her face. "Seeing you makes me yearn for North Forks. I don't have any friends here."

The trip to Northern California had turned into a disaster for Libby. The same seemed true for Mrs. Nolan.

She set her spoon in the tomato soup. "I need to go."

"Go? Where will you go?"

"I'll find a place."

"No, I won't let that happen. Stay the night. Stay as long as you want."

"No, I can't stay."

"Please," she pleaded. "Bill has thrown all his waking hours into work and is rarely home, and Rachael will leave for days. Please, at least for tonight." She could have earned another blue ribbon for the most dramatic personality swap of a lifetime.

By midnight, neither Rachael nor Mr. Nolan had come home. Mrs. Nolan wrapped her arm around Libby's waist as they stepped down a hall to a beautiful guest bedroom with an attached bath.

A portrait of a downcast young girl holding a black cat hung above a cherry wood dresser. The girl had exaggerated dark eyes that stared into the room as if her heart felt as crushed as Libby's. The artist's childlike signature was in the upper right corner—KEANE.

She sat on the bed and closed her eyes, concentrating on the unbearable pain in her chest, mystified at how a heart that had not been physically stabbed or punched, could hurt so much.

Despite her exhaustion, sleep wouldn't come. Each mile of the trip buzzed in her head. Each stop for gas. Each state line and fist of dirt, all to have her 18th birthday destroyed. She took the diary out of her messenger bag. "It looks like you're the only thing I can count on. It's just you and me."

> January 13, 1967—Friday.
> *Yes, Friday the 13th. If I had a gun, I think I'd kill myself. I thought we'd never grow apart. I'm angry. I'm sad. I'm an idiotic fool. I'm alone. I'm afraid. I'm so, so sad.*

In the morning, she brought the Oracle page out of her bag and flinched when she noticed *I miss you* wasn't there like she had remembered. It simply said, "This is where I'll be on your birthday!"

She wrote a short entry before slipping out of the house without a sound, like she had one week earlier in North Forks.

> January 14, 1967—Saturday.
> *Nope, change of thoughts—It's my birthday, and if my mother didn't kill me, I won't let Rachael. I am the only one responsible for my happiness or self-esteem.*

Her first stop was back at the same gas station she had gotten directions before.

"Head to Emeryville, then go West on Hwy 80 across the San Francisco Bay Bridge."

Suspended above the water, she watched small whitecaps flutter below as she drove toward her eighteenth birthday celebration with the sun and Rachael at her back.

Seeing the dramatic San Francisco skyline in front of her, she began to feel better.

# 15

The January sun welcomed the flocks of people moving toward the park for the *Gathering of the Tribes.*

Libby stood to the side, the weight of the past night holding her back until a woman dressed in a pixie costume handed her a strand of beads.

"For you," she said and smiled. "Love beads. Peace."

Alone, yet not, she crossed Lincoln Way toward the Polo Field and walked onto an immense area of flattened grass. Her initial reluctance gave way to excitement as the colorful gathering grew larger.

She heard tinkling bells. The air was crazy with incense and pot smoke and gigantic soap bubbles released from plastic wands.

Girls wearing flowers as hair bands and happiness on their faces skipped around a maypole. Everyone in the park wore kind smiles and beaded necklaces.

Her heart pinched when she impulsively scanned the area for Rachael.

Five girls in matching flower crowns and tie-dye sundresses sat in a circle on the grass. One motioned for Libby to join them. Happy to be invited, she plopped down on the space they cleared.

"It's going to start any minute."

"What?" Libby asked.

The girl pointed toward a flatbed truck. Old rugs and pillows covered the back end.

"There's the stage," she said as five people jumped onto it. Each held an instrument.

One man brought a conch shell to his mouth. A sound similar to a foghorn traveled over the park. The others lowered themselves and sat cross-legged. Libby strained to see over the heads of the people in front of her.

The man with the conch shell, and another in a white robe, began striking small finger cymbals. Soon, they added their voices.

"What are they saying?" Libby asked the girl next to her.

"I think it's a Zen Buddhist chant. Or, Hindu."

"What does it mean?"

The girl shrugged. "I don't really know."

"Who are they?"

"The guy on the left is Gary Snyder, and the one on the right, with the beard, is Ginsberg."

Libby bobbed her head.

"And I'm Hope."

"I'm Libby. Thanks for letting me sit with you." She laughed. "It's my birthday."

Behind the two men chanting, a woman tapped a tambourine against her hip. Another man played a hand rattle. Another cradled an autoharp. As if a mystical force had swept over them, the audience swayed.

All five moved offstage with an understated grace. The mosaic of people gathered erupted in appreciation. Hope took a toke off a tightly rolled joint and handed it to Libby.

"Happy Birthday."

Libby had smoked cigarettes at parties but never marijuana. An intense burn hit her lungs at the first inhale, and she coughed out spastic flutters of smoke. The girls didn't seem to care.

On the second pass, she pulled in evenly, controlling the intake and the exhale. By the third hit, a rush of euphoric dizziness filled her, followed by contentment.

Through a haze, she watched a beautiful man jump onto the stage. He was a modern-day sorcerer dressed in white, with twinkling eyes and floppy flowers tucked over his ears. He took command of the microphone.

"Turn on. Tune in. Drop out." He spoke casually yet full of life. Libby had no idea what he meant.

He brought his hands up. "Drop out of high school, drop out of college, drop out of graduate school, drop out of junior executive, drop out of senior executive." His voice rose. He repeated, "Turn on. Tune in. Drop out."

The man left the stage to thunderous cheers. Libby said to no one, "Drop out of your family. Drop out of North Forks." She leaned toward Hope. "Who was that?"

"Timothy Leary. The king of psychedelics. The acid guru."

Again, Libby wasn't sure what she meant.

Hope tutored her on the San Francisco local bands as they took the stage, announcing their names. Big Brother and the Holding Company, Quicksilver Messenger Service, Blue Cheer. Hope had seen them all at the Fillmore and free "happenings" in the park.

When Hope said, "Jefferson Airplane's next," Libby sat up on high alert, then stood and moved toward the stage, weaving through the crowd, checking face after face. She circled the truck, then circled back. Rachael was nowhere near.

She swerved through hundreds of people dancing wildly and took a few detours before giving up and winding her way back to the girls. Hope gestured for her to hurry.

"The Grateful Dead's next."

"I think I've heard of them."

Their hypnotic rhythm pulsed. Each song went on forever and segued into another. For her, music had usually served as background, but on that day, it became the center of all.

A dark-haired guy wearing a bandana headband walked toward her and offered his hand. Over his fringed jacket, he wore a necklace of silver arrowheads and turquoise beads like the ones she'd seen in New Mexico. A leather boda bag dangled from his shoulder.

His soft eyes were the shade of dried tobacco leaves. They encouraged her to join him. She reached for his hand. They began to move to the music. He leaned into her. "I love these guys. I saw their concert last year at the Fillmore. They're San Francisco royalty."

"What's your name?"

"Gypsy," he said.

As they danced through the day, Libby drifted into an immense calm like she'd never felt before—as if she had found her home.

A bi-plane circled above. A parachutist jumped from its belly and floated into the park like an angel from the sky.

When nearing sunset, a voice from the stage thanked everyone for coming and asked them to face the sun and move toward it.

# 16

Two days had passed since the Be-In, and Libby was still by Gypsy's side. With hands linked, they walked the streets of Haight-Ashbury, the area itching to be part of a revolution.

Gypsy's courting style introduced her to the places he considered authentic "Hashbury." They flipped through the wooden bins of albums lining the walls of Melrose Records. Gypsy plucked out the *Blonde on Blonde* album and brushed the back of his hand across Dylan's scarf.

"Do you know this one?" he asked.

"I know who Dylan is, but not the album. He's from Minnesota. Duluth."

"This album is where rock, or pop as art, started." He set it back in the bin. "Dylan's a top notch poet."

They spent hours in The Blue Unicorn, the famed coffeehouse where artists and students congregated. It claimed to have the cheapest food and coffee in town.

They strolled past small family owned stores and bars, and head shops that also served as unofficial community centers.

She enjoyed being by his side, his arm across her shoulder. Their stride gave life to a comfortable rhythm as they stepped over strung-out addicts and joined impromptu sing-alongs on street corners. The San Francisco scene was so different from her old life that it could have just as easily been the tenth planet in the solar system.

On the back panel of Gypsy's VW bus, he painted a peace sign and stuck a *Killing For Peace is Like Screwing for Virginity* sticker on the bumper. Along the side panels and doors he had used a detailing paint brush to write the lyrics of the ultimate counterculture anthem.

*The eastern world it is explodin' Violence flarin', bullets loadin' You're old enough to kill but not for votin' You don't believe in war, what's that gun you're totin'? And even the Jordan River has bodies floatin But you tell me over and over and over again my friend Ah, you don't believe we're on the eve of destruction. P.F. Sloan.*

Inside the bus, a crocheted granny square blanket covered the mattress taking up the back half. A matted shag carpet and paisley throw pillows filled the space between the bed and the sparse kitchen shelving behind the front seats.

Before Libby met Gypsy, she'd had sex twice with a boy no more experienced than her. Both times were clumsy and rushed, for fear his parents would be home soon. The boy and the sex were disappointing, and neither seemed worth another try. She could never have imagined how this man, Gypsy, would so quickly transform her from girl to woman.

"Be still," he said. "I want to show you how beautiful you are."

His fingertips ignited longings unknown to her before. Together, their moist, earthy odors melted her suit of armor and replaced it with the acceptance of being worthy of desire. Libby was an eager student in the hands of a thoughtful teacher.

She told him about the smallness of North Forks and the freedom she felt while driving cross country. She talked about her dream of reuniting with Rachael, only to have it squashed, and despite that, how determined she was to get to the Be-In for her birthday.

"Meeting you made the day more special," he said. "I came down from Portland for the chance to see Alan Ginsberg."

"The man with the beard and glasses playing the cymbals in the beginning?" she asked, thankful Hope had pointed him out.

"Yes, he's the one." His voice was light. "The beat poets are my heroes. My cosmic guides, you know? Ginsberg, Kerouac, O'Hara. Ever heard of O'Hara?"

Libby shook her head.

"He wrote poetry as smooth as Fred Astaire's dancing." A soft smile formed on his lips.

Her smile mirrored his.

"Man, he made the hard work look easy."

"You really like poetry?" she asked.

"Yes. Even if my words haven't found their way to paper yet, I think of myself as one." He rolled a fresh joint and licked the paper. "They have a poetry reading at the Unicorn every week. I'll take you there on Wednesday."

She had never met anyone as exotic as him. The difference in their age was two years, but he had been raised to question authority and encouraged to travel. Not only was he vehemently opposed to a war she had barely heard of, he was suspicious of the government because of it—foreign concepts to a girl from the North Country.

On their third night together, while smoking a joint and drinking wine from his bota bag, Libby said, "Tell me about your happiest day."

Gypsy kissed the side of her face and said, "I've had a lot of happiest days. How about I tell you about my least happy day? The day I turned from carefree to serious."

"When was that?"

He poured a stream of wine into his mouth and handed her the bota.

"The evening before my eleventh birthday."

"What happened?"

"My dad handed me the rifle his father had once given him." Gypsy's voice tightened. "He said, 'Get a good night's sleep because we're going deer hunting early tomorrow.' I hardly slept from the excitement of sharing the day with him, walking alongside him in the autumn brush, and feeling the rifle's weight across my arms."

"Isn't that what all boys want? To go hunting with their dad? Why was it unhappy?"

He straightened. "We'd been settled in the blind for an hour or so when an eight-point buck moved our way. He stopped in front of us and his soulful eyes looked into mine. I squeezed the trigger and shot him." The sorrow in Gypsy's voice reflected the years of remorse.

"He fell, and I ran to him on the bloody dirt. When he stopped kicking, I put my hand on the oozing hole in his neck." Gypsy stroked the string on the bota bag. "When he was gone, I pulled my hand off his neck and cried." Gypsy took another swig of wine. "That was the day I vowed to never kill again. The look in his eyes comes back to me often."

The people in North Forks revered the practice of shooting animals. It was a noble activity. The Holy Grail of Fall. They prepared their deer stands to ensure an advantage and equipped them with heaters, coolers, and chairs. No matter the size of the deer, elk, pheasant, rabbits—the more they killed, the better.

# 17

At one of the small tables in The Drogstore Cafe, Libby sat across from Gypsy, reflecting on the past six days. He was her new-world mentor in the untamed land of incense, tie-dye, wild music, and the new religion of expanding consciousness with the help of drugs.

The root beer floats they ordered came. Gypsy's shoulder-length hair swung as he stabbed the spoon into his glass. "This place used to be called the Drugstore Cafe," he said laying the spoon on the folded napkin. "Big Brother viewed the name as subversive and slapped all sorts of objections and red tape at their feet."

"Why?"

"Just to mess with them. But instead of caving to the establishment or fighting it, they flipped the script and changed the u to o."

"So, they got 'em back?"

"For now," he said.

She scanned the scene in the cafe, wondering if Rachael had ever been there. At the table to her right, three raggedy guys shared a basket of French fries smothered in catsup and an ashtray overflowing with used-up butts. Libby still hadn't become accustomed to public spaces thick with undertones of weed and the stink of unwashed people.

"Hobos," her mother would have said.

She returned to her foamy root beer and scooped up a bite of ice cream. Gypsy's eyes met hers. "You know, Lib," he said softly, without a hint of what would follow. "These days together have been a cosmic place." He fiddled with the turquoise beads on his necklace. "But I've gotta split back to Portland."

She swallowed the ice cream and held her face still, hoping no one in the cafe heard the noise screeching inside her head.

"Sorry to drop this on you now." He picked at a nick in his fingernail. "But the new semester starts next week, and I need to focus."

Not moving a muscle, she studied the ashtray on the next table, thinking she should have been immune to freight trains crashing into her at full speed by now.

She sucked in a breath and choked out, "Next week?" *What about me?*

"I'm not saying I don't dig spending time with you because I do, but I've gotta stay in school to secure my deferment, and think about my future.

SDS needs all hands on deck. It's too important for distractions like you."

She looked at his face and saw the stranger she had foolishly fallen for, absorbed only in himself.

"Is that what I am? A distraction?" she said, humiliated she meant so little to him.

"Like I said, I'm sorry to hit you with this so late, but we were having such a great time I couldn't bring myself to spoil it."

"Spoil it?" she said flatly.

"Oh, come on, Lib, I'm not one of those guys who treat women as sex objects and toss them aside on a whim. I fell for you, I did, but life is more than romantic feelings. It's about purpose."

Dizzy from the massive blow, she knew she couldn't walk to the front door without stumbling and making a bigger fool of herself. To stall, she pushed the remains of her root beer float over to him.

"Lib," he said. "I don't know where your journey will take you. The two of us meeting was the first step. It's your trip to figure out for yourself." He scooped out some ice cream.

"You say purpose? So, tell me why this anti-war movement is so important to you?"

"Like Steinbeck wrote in *East of Eden*, 'What do I believe in? What must I fight for, and what must I fight against?' My answer is that I believe in this movement because it's morally right, and I must fight against the war for the same reason. It's my calling."

His words weaved in and out of her thoughts. She had nowhere to go and didn't know anyone. She thought if they kept talking, he might change his mind. "I'm all ears."

He waited a moment. "You sure?"

She rubbed her eyes and nodded.

"Well, first thing is, this war is a total betrayal of the principles we were founded on, and straight-up unconstitutional." He put the spoon back in the glass and leaned forward. "Both being huge reasons. But more than that, it's grossly wrong."

A furrow crossed his brow, tightening as he spoke. She hadn't noticed it before, and while studying its angle she missed a part of what he said about Congress not declaring it a war.

"I hate to say," she said, "but I didn't know Congress declared wars."

"Article I, Section 8," he said. "Look it up."

"I will. And I hardly know anything about the war."

"Check that out, too," he said. "How many of our brothers do you think they drafted in the past year?"

She shook her head and shrugged.

"So far, it's over 385,000. Shipped off to a rotten jungle for all the wrong reasons in just one spin around the sun.

"Do you know how many they killed in those same twelve months?" His face, eyes, spirit, and his passion radiated with every word. She recognized what he had meant when quoting Steinbeck.

"No."

"6,000."

A voice behind her yelled, "Right on, man. For what?"

"NOTHING," Gypsy yelled back at him. "Not to mention the 30,000 casualties."

The war had not come up in their past week together. She hadn't seen him this wound-up before. His voice rose.

"If you're not in college, with a deferment, your only smart choice is to move to Canada." She looked around the room and realized everyone's focus was on them.

She thought of the bumper sticker on the ceiling of his van: *When the RICH wage war, it's the POOR who die.*

"Please, no more numbers." Libby wasn't sure which was worse, the horror of his words or the ache in her heart.

"Numbers and language are essential, like the word *conflict*. Vietnam conflict, my ass."

The manager approached the table and asked him to tone it down. He lowered his voice. "Another word they use to mislead us is *casualties*. It sounds benign. To them, having your arm blown off is a casualty. Legs gone. Eyes. Brains."

Seeing her stunned face, he said, "Sorry, sorry. I got way out there."

"What's going on?"

"Sorry," he said again. He spun his chair around and straddled it. "Just like you, I was clueless. I only learned about Vietnam two years ago when a friend told me we were sending troops there. I had to look at a map to see where it was. You know where it is?"

"No," she said, feeling pitifully unaware.

"It's a peanut-sized country some eight thousand miles away. As soon as I saw it, I needed to find out what was going on, and went to a teach-in on my campus. The information I got from that meeting magnified all I had felt. My fate was sealed. SDS was my path."

Liberty took a deep breath and nodded as if she understood. It seemed clear nothing she'd say would keep him in San Francisco. She still wanted to stretch out this last time together, thinking maybe he'd ask her to go to Portland with him.

"What's SDS?"

"Students for a Democratic Society." He went into great detail about the history and goals of the group. "That's another of the many reasons I've got to get back."

His eyes had no trace of their past few days together—only his future.

They drove in silence to Grove Street near Alamo Square, where Sweet Pea was parked. The last wisps of light settled on the horizon as they pulled up. Numbness grew inside her. She slid open the side door and removed the bag her clothes were in.

As she walked toward Sweet Pea, Gypsy stepped out of the van and said, "If you stay in San Francisco, you should change your name to Liberty. It fits you perfectly. You came all this way for the freedom and control of your life." He put up two fingers to form a peace sign. "You'll always be Liberty to me."

She remained on the sidewalk, watching him drive off. *The eastern world it is explodin'.* No, she thought. It's my world that's explodin'.

# 18

# Harper

# 2019

One Saturday morning, while watching a crow circle above Charlotte from the kitchen window, Libby entered my mind like an invisible breeze.

I'd only had the diary a month when Eddie and Vernon both destroyed my life on the same day. After those two episodes, there wasn't an ounce of light-heartedness left in me, and the diary had slipped from my thoughts.

The last I'd read, she was in Glenrio, tasting Mexican food for the first time and working her way to Santa Monica. I fantasized about meeting her at the water's edge—two barefoot friends splashing each other in the Pacific Ocean.

Later that day, under Charlotte's shade, it hit me I'd imagined meeting the young girl, but the reality was that I'd be meeting an old lady.

If Libby was eighteen in 1967, she was born in 1949, and she'd be the same age as my grandparents, if they had made it past the Perry exit.

If still alive, what would she be doing? Living alone? Cooking for grandchildren my age? Or stuck in an old folks' home, playing bingo?

"Oh my God, Charlotte, I'm such an idiot." I leaned back on her trunk. "SUCH an idiot."

The sun flickered between the shifting leaves as if to agree. *I found the diary in Hickory Springs. Right here.* A tingling chill hit my skin. She could be close by.

A squirrel bounced through Charlotte's branches, scolding me with its barking sound and tail flips as if to say, "Harper Warner, get your shit together."


The screen door slammed behind me as I hurried up the ladder to my room. I had hidden the diary from Eddie under the bed in a Tampax box.

When I slipped it out, it looked more fragile and worn than before. I needed to take better care of it. Without a doubt, it deserved a better home then a feminine hygiene box.

Mama was the only one other than me who knew about the diary. *The glass knob on the nightstand drawer was shining like your pendant and begging me to pull it open and take what was inside—like I was chosen to be its keeper. So, how did it end up in that shop?*

When I returned from my daydream, it seemed clear I had to make another trip to the Second Chance, this time with a purpose.

Instead of the old lady with the big dentures, a skinny boy came out from behind the desk. He wore Doc Martens, baggy drawstring pants, and a t-shirt with a picture of Will Smith when he was *The Fresh Prince of Bel-Air.* I smiled on the inside and wanted to say, "Dude, for God's sake, it's 2019."

I'd never seen anyone but old people work in thrift shops—retired people who spent their time volunteering for a good cause, or a church.

"You work here?"

"Sometimes, to help out my grandma."

*Could he be Libby's grandson?*

"Is she okay?"

"She's okay, just under the weather."

"Do you mind telling me her name?"

"Berta. Berta Copeland. Why?"

"It's nothing," I said, feeling like I'd crossed into loony land. "I thought I might know her."

"Shoes and purses are half price today. Items with yellow tags are twenty-five percent off, and everything upstairs is on clearance."

"I'm not looking for shoes." I smiled. "But there's a nightstand with crystal knobs upstairs. Can you tell me how much it is?"

"Let's go up there and take a look," he said optimistically, the way a car salesman does as soon as you step foot on the lot.

He followed me. The toes of his boots banged into each riser, shaking the frail stairway.

At the landing, my heart sank. "It was there last time I came in. Right there, next to the clock." I pointed to the side wall.

"When was that?"

"About a month ago."

"Chances are it might have sold."

"No."

"Don't worry, we have other nightstands." He pointed to a mint green piece of shit.

"No. I told you I need the one with the crystal knobs."

"Think positive," he said, like Libby would have. "Things get moved when they bring new stuff up here. I held my breath when he pushed a big console record player to one side.

"No, it's not here."

He moved past a chubby sofa toward the back wall and peeked behind a bookcase.

"Is this it?"

My foot smacked into a box of old, rusted license plates. I kicked it to the side and rushed to see.

"Yes, yes."

His back stiffened when I hugged him.

"I know you don't care, but this belonged to someone named Libby Carlson."

"A friend of yours?"

"Sort of. It doesn't matter."

We moved a table blocking the way. I trailed him as he shouldered the nightstand down the stairway. My heart jumped each time he banged it into the wall. He set it near the cash register.

"Do you know who donated it?" I asked.

"No. They don't keep those kind of records here."

"How much is it?"

He checked the sides and back. "I don't see a price tag."

The diary didn't have one either.

"Will you take twenty?"

He shook his head and said, "Because this means a lot to you, you can have it for fifteen." I gave him a genuine smile, glad I'd held my tongue about his clothes.

"Here's sixteen."

"This is too much."

"Truth is, I forgot to pay for a book last time I was here."

My quest to reunite the diary and the nightstand was complete. Like a heart and a soul, they belonged together. The gloomy day brightened.


I swiped the cobwebs and dust off the top with a damp wad of paper towels. Three round watermarks rose on the right corner. *Libby's circles?* My fingers traced the scars.

Burned into the back panel was the logo AFR. No clues were pointing to Libby. No secret piece of paper with her recognizable handwriting called out to me. No phone number was etched in the wood.

Uncle Kevin had rigged a rope and pulley for me to haul things upstairs without him. My new purchase looked at home next to my bed. I topped it with Mama's tea towel embroidered with wildflowers, and then I sat on my bed to read a few pages.

After all that time, I hadn't read any further than the middle of January. For sure, a couple sessions with a shrink would reveal I was afraid to move on with my life.

> January 10, 1967—Tuesday
> *Slept in a Wigwam last night. I felt all out of proportion, like Alice in Wonderland. Very tall in my round, concrete teepee. Very small under the starry sky. Very sad about my past. Very happy about my future. Couldn't sleep, do to freight trains, so left early.*

The thing about feeling all out of proportion hit home with me.

> January 11, 1967—Wednesday
> *O glory, glory (corny but true). The Pacific Ocean played its magic on me today. The*

*smell, the size, the colors, and the power. I spent the afternoon and twilight hovering over it at a fantasy land the locals call P.O.P. It's been the best day of my life, with more to come. I'll be with Rachael tomorrow.*

When I turned the page, an itty-bitty ticket, like you get at raffles, was taped to it. Pacific Ocean Park, Inc. General Admission $1.25. Man, I thought, that's how much a small bag of Lay's Classics costs today.

The little ticket, a fifty-year-old leftover from a day of fun and freedom, sent my emotions in the wrong direction. I didn't think I'd ever have a day as nice as that.

When I set the diary inside the nightstand, the drawer stuck, like before.

# 19

The turns and dips on the road to Big Papa's Liquor became all too familiar during those worst six months. Mama, Eddie, Vernon.

Julius worked the register on Tuesdays, Wednesdays, and Thursdays until closing. Without Big Papa there, he turned a blind eye to the laws of selling alcohol to minors. "Howdy" was about all he said unless forced to answer questions.

On the counter in front of Julius was the usual liquor store stuff—5-hour energy shots, lighters, Big Jims, and the credit card machine.

Behind him, the liquor bottles competed for space along glass shelves. They looked like sad little orphans waiting to be picked out of the lineup and taken home.

"Can you get me one of those Southern Comforts? The pint."

He knew what I wanted but didn't reach for it until I asked. Comfort was my drink because of its name, and cheddar cheese Pringles went hand in hand with it. Julius would stuff the bottle and chips in a brown bag and palm my twenty-dollar bill in one motion. He never asked for my I.D., and I knew not to expect change.

Laying on my bed, half a bottle in, the trash cans outside clattered when the wind knocked them over. I cried because I knew how they must have felt. I opened the nightstand drawer, picked up the diary, and released the gold clasp.

> January 15, 1967—Sunday.
> *As far as I know, Rachael didn't come home Friday night. Turns out I don't need her. Entering Golden Gate Park was like entering my future. I met some girls who turned me on to my first joint, and everything changed. And I met Gypsy. There's a whole world out there waiting to have fun, and it chose my birthday to welcome me to join in.*

Like we were best friends, I said, "Good Lord, look what you did, Libby. You're always ready to shake off the bad." I laughed. "Happy Fucking Birthday." Then I added, "Screw the box of chocolates idea," and read straight through to the last word she'd written. When I finished, a lightness washed over me.

Grateful for the relief, I heard Mama's sweet voice in my mind and felt her soft lips against my cheek. And I thought about Libby, who never felt kisses from her mom. We were both motherless, but at least mine had been a good one.

The small part of her life I'd read about inspired me to become as strong and daring as she had been—or at least try. She even changed her name.

For the next week, I thought about the pep talks she gave herself—her magic words. The stuff like, *I am the only one responsible for my happiness*, and *I can't be afraid of being afraid.*

At first, I thought, jibber-jabber. It's like saying you shouldn't let the death of your mother get you down, or you can't let getting fired because you didn't want to go out with the pock faced idiot manager ruin your world. And it didn't seem possible for a regular, everyday person to think or say a sentence and change her frame of mind.

I wondered what wiping pain away with a single thought would be like. It seemed only a superhero could do that, but Libby, I mean Liberty, was a regular girl like me.

I stood in front of my dresser, examining myself in the mirror. With only a sliver of conviction, I said, "Okay, Miss Liberty, let's do this."

My tools were a fine-point Sharpie and a Pop-Up note dispenser. On the first Post-It, I wrote the phrase she repeated often, *I can't let disappointment keep me disappointed,* and slapped it close to the top of the mirror.

*Negative thoughts do not serve me anymore,* and, *My past doesn't predict my future* went on either side of it. Checking the diary, I added eight more, then ended with my favorite: *My life will have meaning.* I arranged them in a circle.

Uncle Kevin had his own twisted version of the power of positive thinking. He once asked me, "Have I ever told you about Shit Pipe Syndrome?"

"Come on, that's not a thing."

"Oh yes, it is. You get it from standing under a shit pipe. And, the longer you stay, the more shit will dump on your head. Once you figure it out," he pointed his finger to his temple. "All it takes is the first step. Either one step to the right or one step to the left. No more shit."

"I'm pretty sure it's you who's full of shit," I said.

Sometimes, I wake up exhausted after having the same dream about driving on a windy road and I can't open my eyes. That night, I climbed into bed thinking about the affirmations on my mirror and ended up inside a watermelon, carefully carving out a set of stairs with two tiny dental picks. One pick fell to the bottom of the staircase. With only one left, the effort to crawl up each step and carve another was exhausting. When I reached the green rind door, The Statue of Liberty opened it and offered her hand to help me break free. *Liberty.*

As if the cloud of doom had lifted, the ache of missing Mama was manageable. Energized, I Googled how to submit a harassment complaint and found I was still within a 180-day window since the *incident* happened. Instead of navigating through all the formal bureaucracy on the website, I called Hickory Springs Hardware and asked to speak with Mr. Wyatt.

# 20

I sat in a wooden chair on the visitor side of old man Wyatt's desk in an office smelling like decades of stale cigar smoke.

Generations of Hickory Springs Hardware calendars, set on the month of January, covered all four walls. Each had a picture of a location around town.

Mr. Wyatt's bulk filled his worn leather chair. His eyes glistened under heavy lids, and his oversized ears put me at ease with the possibility he'd be a good listener.

"Miss Warner, I understand you're here about your termination."

"Yes sir, I am." I hesitated, not knowing where to start. My nerves got the best of me and I blurted out, "Mr. Wyatt, have you ever heard of a condition called Shit Pipe Syndrome?"

"No," he said with a smile. "But I'm guessing you'll tell me about it."

Once I explained the premise to him, my nerves settled.

"Sitting here with you is my first attempt at stepping out from under the pipe because I believe I was wrongfully let go."

Mr. Wyatt let me blabber on like a ninny about when Vernon asked me out and my last day in the lunch room. I ran out of words and posed the question, "Would you want to go out with him?"

"He's not exactly my type," he said. "But, before we go any further with hypothetical's, let me tell you, I looked into Mr. Montgomery's shenanigans and fired his ass."

It took me a few seconds to process his words. "You fired him? So, he doesn't work here anymore?"

"That's what it means." He smiled and folded his arms over his belly. "I usually leave personnel decisions up to my managers, and wasn't aware of the circumstances of your termination until my secretary told me about your phone call." Mr. Wyatt looked to be enjoying himself. "It turns out Mr. Montgomery had committed quite a few, shall we call them indiscretions."

"Oh, thank you, Mr. Wyatt. I was afraid you wouldn't believe me because I waited so long."

"One thing I know for sure." He nodded as if to agree with himself. "Truth doesn't have an expiration date. And it's you who should be thanked."

"Me?"

"Yep. I discovered more than I wanted. That disrespectful thief won't work in this town again."

"Thief?"

"Pilferer. Shoplifter. Cheat. Pick a word."

"Wow," was the only word I came up with.

"If not for your phone call, who knows how long he'd have gotten away with his wrongdoings."

My mind spooled back to all the times I had been timid and stayed under the pipe.

"So, Mr. Wyatt, can I have my job back?"

"If you want it back, it's yours."

"Can I have more hours?"

"If you want 'em, you've got 'em."

"How about a raise?"

"You've gotta earn that."

With our time winding down, I had one more question. "How many calendars are here?"

"There's sixty-five years of Hickory Springs history on these walls."

"How come they're all turned to January?"

"My dad kept them that way, and I've followed his lead. He believed it was the most hopeful month, with new beginnings and all."

"Nice," I said, to be polite. Truth be, the month of January had betrayed me more than once.


After the meeting with Mr. Wyatt, I lost the craving to pour Southern Comfort into my morning coffee, and positive thoughts worked their way into my days. Life seemed to be looking up until I got Uncle Kevin's text in the middle of the day.

*Come 2 my place aftr school*

> *Wts up*

*Nt urgent.*

> *WHAT?*

*@ my place*


He handed me an unopened envelope with a round logo. State Of Georgia, Division of Family and Child Protective Services.

I searched his face for an explanation, only to see confusion.

"What do you think they want?"

He shook his head. "I don't know. Can't be good."

"Should we open it?"

He sucked air in through his teeth. "Guess we don't have much of a choice."

He read the matter-of-fact letter out loud. It informed us we had an in-home visit with a CPS social worker named Miss Washington, scheduled at 4:30 on Thursday, August 8, 2019.


Thunderstorms and heavy rain let loose on the night of August 7th and throughout the 8th. Uncle Kevin left work two hours before the meeting time. He vacuumed the rugs and emptied the waste baskets while I tossed out the extra cans and bottles left out on the kitchen countertops.

He paced and fidgeted like a third grader. I watched the rain bounce off the stepping stones and chewed off all the progress I'd made on my fingernails.

Her gray Ford Bronco rolled up the drive right on time. Peeking from the side window, I watched the woman maneuver out of the SUV. Her skinny body and long pony-thin legs reminded me of Popeye's girlfriend, Olive Oyl, only Miss Washington was black.

She held a denim briefcase above her head to shield herself from the rain. Her dark, springy hair bounced with each stride up the path. Like in a horror movie, when her knuckles rapped on the door, a lightning bolt struck the sky.

She stepped inside and wiped her shoes on the towel by the door, then set the briefcase next to her leg and offered to shake his hand, then mine.

Her teeth poked out of her mouth when she smiled and said, "Your hair is beyond gorgeous."

I figured the compliment was a tactic to butter me up.

"Thank you."

"I'm Deja. Deja Washington."

The denim briefcase matched her blue jean dress with a bib and suspenders like it wanted to be overalls. One of the straps had a *Black Lives Matter* button pinned to it.

Mama bought a *Black Lives Matter* bumper sticker after we saw Philando Castile get shot five times inside his car. We watched him die, not in real life, but on the news.

Mama kept shaking her head. "This makes me sick."

"Me, too," I said, feeling more scared than sick.

"I don't know what to do, but I need to do something."

"Like what, Mama?"

Her face strained. "I'm not sure."

She had always been troubled with the idea of inequality. Atticus saw to that when he said, "You never really understand a person until you consider things from his point of view..."

Hickory Springs didn't lean toward social justice issues. Just the same, she went on Amazon and ordered a Black Lives Matter sticker with a fist to the right of the words.

She had me peel off the backing and press it onto the bumper. I felt proud every time we drove around town, showing off our support for the wrong done to Philando.

Uncle Kevin offered Miss Washington a seat in the rocker across from the couch where he and I sat, tense and uneasy. After a brief introduction she said she'd been with CPS for five years and looked forward to working with us. She pulled a stack of papers from her bag and set them on the coffee table. Yellow tabs stuck out from the pile, like a set of bad teeth.

"We'll get the essential paperwork out of the way, Mr. Warner."

"Kevin," he said.

She flipped through the papers, stopping at each marked page, briefly explaining the essence of the sections—arbitration, consent, liability, etc. Her long, manicured fingernail pointed to the place Uncle Kevin was to sign.

My body tensed as I watched him scribble his name without reading a word. *Was he signing me away? Was he giving her permission to change our lives? Was he in on this?*

After she said, "And this here is the last one," she pulled another stack of papers out of her case. My chest itched. I clutched the front of my shirt and tugged on it.

"Why are you here? What is this all about?"

"I'm here to assess your living situation and determine if this is the best place for you."

"Where else would I live?" I studied her corkscrew hair and small eyes, then swung my arm back and forth, pointing across the room. "I live here. Right here."

Uncle Kevin cleared his throat and scooted to the front of the couch. "Miss Washington." He flashed his best smile. "I know you mean well, and we really appreciate you coming all the way out here." He patted my shoulder. "The thing is, she's been through a lot, and this visit is unnecessary. I'm sure you know Harper will be eighteen in five months."

"Yes, I understand."

"My sister and I went through a great deal of needless harassment from Social Services when our parents died back in the eighties. I'm here to see it doesn't happen to Harper."

Deja Washington shifted her attention to me.

"I'm sorry for what must seem like an intrusion, but my hands are tied. This first visit is mandatory to capture information for the record."

"Who's record? What kind of information? What happens to it?" I challenged.

"The basics. Finance, education, opinions."

The interrogation began with yes and no questions printed on official CPS forms. As we answered, she marked a large black X in the appropriate square. Yes. Yes. No. Yes. Stupid, redundant, none-of-your-business answers.

"Now, Mr. Warner." She flashed her extra white teeth.

"Kevin," he said forcefully.

"Sorry. Kevin," she repeated. "Since Harper is in your care, I must ask if you're in a committed relationship."

"You have to ask me if I'm in a committed relationship?" he said through a laugh. "Why?"

She pressed her lips together.

My mind whirled. *Did she want this information for CPS, or for herself? Was she flirting with him?* The thought was too much. I waited for his answer.

"The word committed is a tricky one," he said. "Can you please describe your definition of it?" He didn't wait for an answer. "Never mind. I know what it means, and no, Miss Washington, I am not."

"Sorry, but I have to ask. Do you sometimes have your dates come here?"

He chewed on his mustache. "No, Miss Washington. I've been completely devoted to taking care of Harper since she came to live here."

When she asked if he drank or did drugs, he stayed cool, cool, cool, and again, lied like a proper gentleman.

Uncle Kevin wasn't movie star good-looking, but the combination of his rumpled blond hair and chunky mustache gave him a rugged look. As gentle and resourceful as he was, I often wondered why he hadn't settled down with one woman. His relationships never seemed to evolve into more than a crazy quilt of temporary satisfactions.

Mama used to say he was a catch-and-release man. A part of me was content with having him to myself, but I still thought he should settle with someone.


Deja Washington gathered all the papers that had to do with my future and slipped them into the denim bag.

"For the record," she said. "My job is to listen. It's the most important thing I can do. Our goal at

CPS is to keep the family together, and we're generally successful."

"Since it's your job to listen," Uncle Kevin said. "I want you to know, for the record, I think your trip out here today has been senseless, and a form of harassment. The most important thing I have to do is take care of my niece, and this, whatever you call it, brought a boatload of stress to her. Like I said before, she'll age out in five months."

"I understand," she said. "If you need anything I can help you with, say the word."

We both nodded. For the first time since the letter had arrived, I calmed down. Her *Black Lives Matter* pin came loose from her strap and settled in her lap.

"Did you get that online?" I asked.

"No. They have an office in Atlanta. I got it there." She tossed it to me. "Keep it. I have plenty more."

"How come you went all the way to Atlanta to get it?"

"I volunteer there on weekends."

"What do you do?"

"Whatever they need, from monitoring the comments on the website to walking door to door and talking to people."

"Do you like it?"

She shook her head. "It shouldn't even exist. But it's essential." She laughed. "Don't get me started, Harper. My passion runs deep."

When she stood to leave, she reached into her purse and said, "You're required to have a session with a licensed psychologist before I can make my recommendations. I like to use Dr. Landry for my cases. He'll be open and fair in his assessment of your living situation." She handed me his business card.

An embossed, round, county seal popped out on the backside. The front had a mess of degrees and initials after his name. A hum filled my head as I ran my finger over the raised circle of judgment.

"Harper," Deja Washington said.

When there was no response, she said, "His office will call you with an appointment time and date."

"I'm tired. Can we be done now?"

She answered with a soft voice. "Yes."

The Bronco's tires spun in the gravel as it backed out of the drive.

Exhausted, I opened the nightstand drawer and put Deja Washington's BLM button next to the diary.

# 21

I was halfway through a *Law and Order SVU* rerun, when Uncle Kevin rapped "Shave and a Haircut, Two Bits" on my door.

Just before I paused the television, Olivia told Stabler he had an anger management problem, like his rages were something new.

I opened the door. "What's up?"

"Deja Washington called. She's coming out here tomorrow."

"What? Hold up. Seriously? Tomorrow? No warning? Can she do that?"

He put the palm of his hand toward my face to say stop. "I told her it would be fine."

"It's not fine. I'd say it's the shits." I didn't ask him inside. "How long has it been since the last time?"

"A little over a month."

"It's rude. She can't just show up like she owns the place. We haven't even heard from the shrink yet."

"I've been thinking. It might be to our advantage to treat her nice. She could end up being a friend to us if we let her."

"A friend? You want to be her buddy?"

"You know the saying? The one about getting more with honey than vinegar."

"Yep, I know it. It's about flies. Or is it about rats?"

"Come on, Harper."

If there was ever a black Cinderella story, Deja Washington could have played the lead. She stepped out of the Bronco, looking like a movie star, ready to walk the red carpet. Uncle Kevin had the door open before she got up the porch steps.

"You look like an African princess," he said.

She laughed as she entered the house. "Thank you, Kevin."

"Yes, ma'am, an African princess. And, that's some dress."

*Pour on the honey.*

She had on a cobalt blue African print dress splashed with yellow peacock feathers. A matching headscarf tied into a high knot concealed her wild hair. Hoop earrings the size of bracelets dangled from her lobes, and deep red lipstick popped from her face.

"It's called a Boubou," she said. "They wear them in Senegal at festivals and special occasions."

"We're flattered you consider us a special occasion," Uncle Kevin said, his face downright goofy.

I gave him my *you're really lame* look.

"Well, I'm definitely overdressed for this visit," she said. "But from here, I'm heading to Peachtree Plaza with a girlfriend who's being honored at the Atlanta Black Professionals awards banquet. I'm so proud of her."

Uncle Kevin gestured for her to have a seat. She settled in the rocker. No briefcase in sight.

Having halfway signed off on his *you-get-more-with-honey* philosophy, I asked if she would like a glass of sweet tea.

"Yes, thank you."

I moved slowly into the kitchen, with my ears on alert to be sure they weren't talking about me. I heard Deja Washington say, "Julio Jones is on track to overtake Jerry Rice's record in receiving yards. I'm sure of it."

"I agree," Uncle Kevin said. "It could be before the end of the season. Go Falcons."

I breathed easy and got busy with the ice cubes. When I returned with the tea, there was silence. Her finger scrolled over the screen on her phone. "Here he is." She handed the phone to Uncle Kevin and looked at me.

"I wanted to show him a picture of Cannoli."

I smiled, confused.

"There's two more, Kevin," she said. "Just swipe up."

"From where?" I asked, figuring they were pictures of food. When he passed the phone to me, I saw that her Cannoli was a dachshund. The fattest wiener dog I'd ever set eyes on.

My right leg bounced as I waited for the elephant in the room to shit on my head—the appointment with Dr. Theodor Landry, M.S. LPS-S.

She smiled at me. "Harper, living with your uncle has been good for you?"

"I *can't* live anywhere else."

"I know."

She set her glass on the coffee table. "The truth is, this visit is my last. Instead of a follow-up, this is more of a courtesy call."

"What's going on?" Uncle Kevin asked.

"I gave my notice to CPS and will be leaving at the end of next week."

"How come you're here if you quit?" I asked. "And why didn't they send someone else out? Did you get, like, fired?"

Her lips puckered. "That's a lot of questions, girl. I'll take them one at a time."

Her phone dinged. She ignored it.

"During our visit last month, Kevin noted you had five months left before turning eighteen. So, now there are only four months left. I know you will do just fine without all the unnecessary bureaucratic interference. This is for your ears only," she said to us.

"Noted," Uncle Kevin said.

"I took the unauthorized liberty of inputting a temporary postponement date in your case file for next March. Come then, you'll have aged out, but still be in the system, and there's nothing anybody can do."

"What are you saying?" Uncle Kevin asked. "You're saying it's over?"

"Yes, I'm saying it's over."

"No appointment with the shrink?" I asked.

"No appointment," she assured.

My hands trembled. My voice croaked, "Thank you."

The light hit her face, and pure joy beamed from her toothy smile. In her fancy dress she looked more like royalty from an exotic world of kindness and grace than a civil servant.

"Not like it's anybody's business," I said, "but I'm wondering why you left your job."

She tilted her chin and took a slow breath. "It's been over three and a half years coming." Her dark eyes held mine. "That's how long it's been since they murdered my brother."

My forehead pinched involuntarily.

"Jackson Washington," she said with force. "Remember his name."

I pressed my back against the couch, tight with anticipation of what she'd say next.

"He was on his way to work, same as every morning. According to the police report, two cops pulled him over for a busted tail light."

"Shit." I shook my head. I already knew.

"On Tuesday, April 12th, 2016, Jackson was driving to work, minding his own business." She tightened her lips. "When he stepped out of the car, with his hands in the air, they said he was reaching for a gun, and they shot him. Neither one of their body cams were on."

"Oh, my God."

"It was less than three months after they killed Philando Castile in his car."

Stunned by hearing his name again, I blurted out, "Mama and I saw it on TV." Then I felt like a foolish, immature, insensitive, idiotic little girl.

"If the body cams were off, how do you know it was the police who shot him?" Uncle Kevin asked.

"Cop bullets. And eyewitnesses. But no one on the streets took video of his hands up, or his body jerking from the gunshots, or the cops running everyone off. For all I know, they might have busted the tail light as a cover-up."

Her hands joined in a tight ball. She glanced out the window. "Jackson was a good brother. And a good man." She relaxed her hands. "And a year later, the officers got off."

Wrapped up in her sadness, I couldn't think of anything meaningful to say.

"After three and a half years of rage, I had to do something. The something was to join the Black Lives Matter movement." She added, "Being proactive helps a lot. I've learned that ordinary people attempting to do extraordinary things can make all the difference. The movement is growing as fast as can be. There are twenty-seven chapters in the U.S."

She checked her phone. "Now, I need to leave soon, so let's get back to the business of you."

"I thought we were through. " I said.

"Yes, we're through with the good news, but I also came to tell you about a quirky requirement for extending your Survivors' Benefits until your nineteenth birthday. Since you're still in the system, it applies to you.

"What's that?" Uncle Kevin said.

She warned me not to register for any college classes until after my nineteenth birthday, or risk forfeiting a whole year of benefits.

"It's contrary to common logic because the goal is to help you be self-sufficient. This catch-22 is a prime example of the crazy part of bureaucracies."

Uncle Kevin inhaled deeply and looked skeptical. "We had planned on her going to Community College this first year."

"You would have received this information if I hadn't—you know, what I did. That's why I came here, to make sure you understand your options. The extra year adds up to a lot of money."

"Thank you," I said, having rarely felt those two words more genuinely.

We all stood. She wrapped her arms around me. Her long, tight embrace felt like a dose of penicillin easing an infection.

As she opened the screen door to leave, she turned back and handed me a piece of paper. "This is my cell number and my address in Atlanta. Call me for anything."

Uncle Kevin walked her to her car. Before the driver's door closed, I heard her say, "You're good people."

With Community College more than a year away, Mr. Wyatt gave me a full five-day schedule and came through with a small raise. I talked LeRoy into hiring me to hostess at the The Blue Rooster two evenings a week.

"Are you sure?" Uncle Kevin said. "It might bring back memories."

"No, I'm good. Besides, I practically grew up in the place. It will be my little way of honoring her."

The diner had its own soundtrack. The griddle sizzled and buzzed like a hot jazz solo. LeRoy called out the orders with the baritone voice of an opera superstar demanding center stage. The sounds of the area by the wash basin varied, depending on whose shift it was.

Three weeks in, I felt confident with verifying reservations, seating rotations, chatting with the customers, and my other duties as Evening Hostess. Mama's friend Joanne came through the front door in her trademark floppy green hat and purple glasses. The sight of her hit me with a sudden ache so intense my knees buckled. I swallowed hard and tried to breath naturally. *I miss Mama so much.*

I set the menus on the hostess table, left Joanne standing alone, and shuffled to the bathroom to sit in the stall and wait for the pain to pass. It wasn't long before the doorknob rattled and turned.

"In a minute," I yelled, with no intention of leaving.

Maybe ten minutes later, LeRoy rapped on the door. "Harper," he said. "Take all the time you need."

"I miss her so much," I moaned. "I miss my mama."

"It's okay, girl," he said. "Go on home when you're done in there."

"You're not firing me, are you?"

"No such thing. I know about grief. It's a sneaky bastard and it shows up when you're not expecting. You'll feel better. It just takes time."

# 22

# Liberty

# 1967

She watched the taillights on Gypsy's van get smaller, then fade away.

The heaviness caused by how he so easily moved on settled in like it had nowhere else to be. With nothing to do, she crawled into Sweet Pea's back bench and tucked herself into the sleeping bag.

The January wind blew through the car's thin shell and inflated her sense of doom. *What have I gotten myself into?* The past eight days churned inside her head. She dabbed her eyes with the corner of the sleeping bag and reached for the diary.

"Here we are again. Just you and me."

> January 21, 1967—Saturday
> *First, Rachael treated me like I'm not worth her time, and now him. This*

*was the closest I've come to feeling love. I'm alone and scared. At least it's not snowing. I've gotten to this magically forsaken place and need to figure out what to do next. I have $225.37 left and no place to stay. Even though nothing has worked out for me so far, except my beautiful birthday, I must stay positive. I can't let disappointment keep me disappointed.*

She set the book down and concentrated only on her heartbeat and how evenly it pumped despite the pain, and surrendered to her tears.

Daylight came fast but did little to thaw her bones. She cursed the damp weather, then caught herself. *How could my Minnesota blood thin that quickly?*

Gypsy had made it clear he was moving on, but his parting words had remained through the night. "You should change your name to Liberty. It fits you perfectly."

Taking a different name had never occurred to her before. Why would it? But it made sense to have a new name to go with a new life. A personal gift from her first real love—and her mother would hate it.

January 22, 1967—Sunday

*Slept in Sweet Pea last night. This morning, I felt bad about Gypsy, but not like I should. I can't stop thinking about how our talks woke me up to what's happening in our country and how unaware I would be if I hadn't left home. He opened my mind to new thoughts and possibilities.*

*My heart is aching, but thanks to him, Libby is dead, and Liberty has to make her own way. I vow to you, diary, from now on, my life will have meaning.*

*MY LIFE WILL HAVE MEANING!*

She wrestled herself out of the sleeping bag before moving up front to start the car and crank open the heater knob.

A woman clutching an overstuffed tote opened the front door of the building next to Sweet Pea's parking spot and cautiously moved down the concrete steps. Once she hit the sidewalk, Liberty's attention heightened as she moved past with hips swaying and feet pointing slightly outward, the same way her mother walked. *Is she worried? Does she miss me?* Liberty knew the answer.

As thoughts of her mother lingered, a parking cop walked up and tapped on the car window. Liberty cranked the knob to roll it down. The woman studied the contents inside. "Are you living in your car?"

"No. Just last night."

"Move along, and don't park here again. You're a long way from home." She banged her hand on Sweet Pea's roof above Liberty's head. "Find yourself a safe place to stay, or better yet, go back to Minnesota."

"Thank you, officer."

She tapped the belly of the Christopher doll and watched it bounce around the rearview mirror. *I can't go back.*


Gas prices had gone up three cents a gallon since she was on the road. While the Texaco service attendant pumped ten gallons into Sweet Pea's belly, Liberty washed up and changed clothes in the bathroom.

Her idea of returning to the Blue Unicorn for a cheap breakfast of eggs, scrambled, and rye toast did not go as planned. The toast came burnt and the eggs were overcooked. Listening in on bits and pieces of conversations similar to those she'd had with Gypsy darkened her mood. She willed herself to block out the noise and think about what would come next.

Since she and Gypsy had stayed mainly in the Haight-Ashbury community, it was time to escape the crowded sidewalks of drop-outs and stoners and see some of the shiny parts of San Francisco—the places on the postcards.

Liberty stepped outside just as a Grey Lines tour bus came to a complete stop. The people inside snapped pictures of the hippies on the street like they were on a photographic safari, capturing native wildlife in its habitat from the safety of their oversized vehicle. From the sidewalk, two guys mooned the bus.

She walked down Ashbury toward the panhandle, then turned left or right at will. Her pace quickened when the frenzied clang of a bell and the rattle of whirring cables called for her attention. Clogged with people latched onto the side poles, the Powel and Hyde cable car clanked past, and she thought, *this is San Francisco.*

By mid-afternoon, she reached the Filbert Street steps that hugged the cliff to Telegraph Hill. A sign said *Stairs to Coit Tower.* Each flight of the narrow stairway led to a landing where she stopped to marvel at the shrubbery, still green in January.

At the summit, a white concrete column rose from the tree-covered hillside. Inside the entrance, a colorful world of enormous paintings depicting everyday life in an earlier time, dominated the walls. Murals of farmers and factory workers shared space with poor tent dwellers and women working on an assembly line. A plaque high above each piece gave the name of the work, and the artist.

She climbed the thirteen flights of stairs to the observation deck, steadying herself against the wall to catch her breath. The smells of the city drifted up to greet her from the masterful mosaic of life that served as home to hundreds of thousands of people.

On Russian Hill, the twisty brick road called Lombard Street looked like a page out of a storybook. From the other side of the tower, the low clouds brushed the bottom of the bridge spanning the Golden Gate Straight.

She inhaled the tang of salt air and watched a tour boat vanish behind the pearly light of a cloudbank toward Alcatraz. *I drove out of North Forks and disappeared just like that boat.*

On Washington, past Alta Plaza Park, she passed old mansions thick with concrete, the size of office buildings. A blanket of yellow leaves dropped from Ginkgo trees and cushioned her steps. Lost in thoughts of Dorothy's yellow-brick road, she barely heard the rushed footsteps pounding the pavement behind.

Two men overtook her, one on each side, pressing against each of her shoulders. Their arms slipped through hers and tightened. The stink of piss and weed came with them.

"Nice tittys," the one on her right said and made a smacking sound with his lips. "Wouldn't you say so, Marley?"

Marley laughed like he just heard a joke and leaned in, unsteady. He wiggled the tip of his tongue against her neck, then licked. His teeth grazed her skin. Her vision blurred, and her muscles locked.

She instinctively planted her feet on the sidewalk and wrenched herself out of their grip. A high-pitched war cry lifted from her chest. She rushed at him. "You're disgusting, you pig."

"Be cool, Bitch," Marley said, and reached for her arm. She yanked it back.

With adrenalin exploding from every pore, she shoved the heel of her palm between the upper lip and nose. "Get away from me," she yelled and hit him again in the same spot.

"Hey, hey." Marley cupped his hands to catch the blood. "You broke my nose, Bitch." Blood drops fell to the sidewalk.

"Not cool, cunt," his buddy yelled and rushed toward her.

In the middle of the afternoon, on a street that should have been safe, she swung at the second guy's stomach with both hands tucked in a ball, alternating, not stopping. "Get away," she screamed with each swing.

"Stop, you Bitch." He brought his arms up to protect his sunken torso and backed up. He lost his balance and twisted to catch himself, and his head hit the concrete.

Teeth clenched and heart hammering, Liberty ran to the next corner before stopping to look back. Bent over, with her hands on her knees, she gasped breaths of fear.

Marley sat cross-legged on the sidewalk, still holding his nose. The other one was on his back in the same spot where he fell. Her breathing slowed when a police car pulled up beside the two stoners sprawled on the sidewalk. After a short visit with the cops, Marley and his friend were cuffed and put into the back of the car.

Shook to tears, it took time to let go of the fear. When with Gypsy, she hadn't thought about the dangers of the city or letting her guard down. Her perception of safety had just altered.

# 23

Still trembling from the attack, Liberty rubbed her palm as she moved slowly back toward Haight Street, where she had seen *rooms for rent* signs on bulletin boards in the head shops.

When she turned on Webster heading toward Geary, a commotion echoed through the air. Powerful voices erupted in a purposeful rhythm. She walked to the next intersection and stood behind a collection of onlookers.

On the cross street, protesters marched shoulder to shoulder, curb to curb. A moving procession of families with babies in strollers and young counterculture types in tie-dye, walked alongside men in suits. Rabbis and old ladies locked arms with veterans. The kaleidoscope of humanity carried signs. So many she couldn't read them all. *Another Family for Peace, Johnson is a War Criminal, Don't Kill Our Boys.* Seeing hundreds of people as passionately against the war as Gypsy struck her at her core.

A gust of air hit her face when the flatbed from the Be-In inched past, crammed with musicians and all their gear.

*And it's five, six, seven,*

*Open up the pearly gates,*

The barefoot woman standing next to her sang along.

*Well, there ain't no time to*

*wonder why,*

*Whoopee! We're all gonna die.*

The pain in Liberty's hand lessened, and the sight of the protest dulled her earlier panic. She pushed her way to the front of the curb. To the left, a floppy-haired kid in the middle of the street held a *Hell No, I Won't Go* sign. Around his neck, an oversized peace symbol dangled from a thick chain. He looked younger than her. She guessed around fifteen. He pivoted to the sidewalk and stopped in front of her.

"Come on, man. You don't want to stand on the sidelines."

She stepped off the curb. "You're right."

A yellow biplane flew over the marchers with a banner in tow. It said, *My son was killed in Vietnam. What for?* Emotions coursed through her like a slow-moving stew.

Together, they walked among the other people galvanized to do something. Over a rise, as far as Liberty could see, heads bobbed, and clouds of warm breath floated off with the breeze.

She hadn't been raised to value or need a purpose, and never before would she have grasped its importance. The approving glance of the kid next to her served up a sense of belonging.

The march ended at Union Square. She and the boy walked to the grassy section by The Dewey Monument. She leaned against the base of the column that anchored the Goddess of Victory, and she thought of Gypsy. The seeds he had planted were already sprouting.

With an enthusiastic handshake, the kid said, "By the way, I'm Stuart."

"Nice to meet you, Stuart. I'm Liberty."

"Really?"

She shrugged. "Since this morning."

He scanned the square. "I started out with my sister and her friend but haven't seen them since Divisadero Street. Thought for sure they'd be here."

Despite her sore feet, the exhilaration of what she had just experienced overpowered the thoughts of what happened with Marley, or of going to the head shops to look for a room.

"I'll stay with you until she shows up."

Liberty slid down the side of the monument to the ground and sat with her arms wrapped around her knees. Stuart joined her.

"Is she your older sister or younger?"

"Older."

Beneath the open sky, they talked until the sun faded and the temperature dipped. She told him about her cross-country trip and how different San Francisco is from North Forks. Before she got to the part about Gypsy and the attack earlier, Stuart said, "My family's lived in San Francisco for four generations. My grandparents were from old money."

"What's old money?"

"Really, really rich. My dad says too rich. He leans progressive. I don't know what happened, but they lost most of it and only had three houses left when they died."

"They owned three houses?"

"My folks sold two of them and gutted the insides of the third." He smiled, his eyes fixed on a Dalmatian scratching at a patch of grass. "And converted it into apartments. Andrea and Sunshine rent one of them. Sort of. They pay like a dollar a month. Like, fifty cents each."

"Must be nice."

"They go to Stanford. Both of them are super smart."

"Which one's your sister?"

"Andrea. Her friend is Sunshine. Her real name's Darleen."

"My real name's Libby. My real, real name is Elizabeth."

"I'm pretty sure I'll always be Stuart."

"Where do you think they are?"

He shrugged. "No clue. I figured they'd meet me here. Maybe they went back to their place."

"Where is that?"

"On Baker. Not far from here."

"So, where do you live?"

"With my parents out in Pacifica. I'm staying with Andrea this weekend."

"It was nice meeting you," Liberty said. "Which way is the Blue Unicorn?"

Stuart pointed. "That way. It's a trek from here."

"I left my car there this morning. And I need to find a place to stay or spend another night in the back seat, if you can call it a back seat."

"Why?"

"It's a long story. I need to get going."

"No, come with me to my sister's place. One of them can drive you to your car."

# 24

As they walked, Stuart leaned forward with his fists tucked into his armpits.

"It doesn't look like your shirt is a match for this wind."

"It's a Pendleton," he said. His reply made no sense to her.

"Where I come from, this is spring weather."

"No wonder you left."

Twilight hit the horizon, and towers glistened in the distance. Bay windows popped from the houses along the street and came alive with a welcoming glow.

"They look like doll houses attached to the homes," she said.

Stuart looked up. "I never saw them like that before. Haven't paid too much attention."

A foghorn bellowed two short blasts in the distance. Liberty's eyes widened. Stuart laughed. "You'll get used to those in no time. Sometimes, when the marine layer is just right, you can hear them from twenty miles away."

She liked his easygoing, upbeat way.

"So, why did you pick me to march with you?"

"I could see it on your face."

"What?"

"You wanted to come to the party, and all you needed was an invitation." He tugged on his peace sign necklace. "That, and my sister bailed on me."

He released his hands from his armpits. "Our street is two more blocks."

They turned right on Baker and stopped in front of a beautiful three-story Victorian house wrapped in blue scalloped shingles. She thought they looked like motionless fish scales.

"This was your grandparent's place?"

He nodded. "One of them."

They walked up twelve steps to an enormous wooden porch with a hanging lantern shining above the front door. After climbing two narrow sets of stairs to the third-floor landing, Stuart led her down a small hallway, then into a warm living room.

A blonde and a brunette sat in oversized beanbag chairs made from denim fabric. They were watching *The Dating Game* on a walnut console TV. Three identical chairs were collapsed on the wooden floor.

"Where have you been?" asked the brunette, who looked remarkably like Stuart.

"Where have you been?" he said back. "I was looking for you, waiting for you, but you vanished."

"I stepped on a beer can in the street and twisted my ankle," the blonde said. "I had to sit on the curb until the pain stopped."

The brunette said, "We got tired of watching from the sidelines and came home to get high."

"What about me?"

"You're a big boy. Anyway, we're all here now."

"This is Liberty," Stuart said. "She left home by herself."

Liberty raised her hand as if to say hi.

"This is my sister, Andrea." The brunette waved. "And Sunshine." The blonde did little more than nod.

Their stony reception made Liberty feel awkward, and she questioned why she had gone with Stuart in the first place.

He plopped in one of the empty beanbags. "Chill," he said, pointing to the bag beside him. She took off her coat and sat.

"Liberty was a protest virgin before today, thanks to me," he said.

"Far out," Sunshine said. "A first timer? What'd you think?"

"It was the best thing I've done in my life. I felt like I belonged. I felt like today was the reason I left home."

"Okay, be quiet," Sunshine said. "*The Honeymooners* is on next. Shelia MacRae's the new Alice. She and Gordon got divorced."

"Speak English, Sunshine," Stuart said.

"Gordon MacRae. You know, Billy Bigelow in Carousel. Curly from Oklahoma."

"Um," Liberty said as she jiggled her butt to rearrange the beans around it. "Are you talking about movies?"

"She's from Los Angeles, or should I say Haaaallywood," Stuart said. "Her dad's a big Haaaallywood producer, but she's not always like this. It's the weed. Makes her name-drop."

"Shut up, Stuart. I'm not name-dropping. I went to school with Heather. Name-dropping is when you don't know the people."

"It's still name-dropping. Anyway, who's Heather?"

"Their daughter."

"Whose daughter?"

"Never mind."

The room's warmth lulled Liberty to sleep. When she woke to the smell of pot, a girl on the television holding a surfboard was running along the beach, advertising Summer Blonde hair lightener.

Stuart leaned against the wall, smoking a joint. He offered her a toke. "A friend with weed is a friend indeed," he said while sitting back down next to her.

Liberty took a drag and stretched to hand it back. "Thanks."

She hadn't said more than ten words since entering the apartment, and nobody seemed to notice or care.

After a second joint had been passed around, Andrea and Sunshine's became more friendly. As soon as *The Lawrence Welk Show* came on, Sunshine went over to the television and turned it off.

"Okay, tell us the story of your life," she said. "Stuart said you left home. From where? And why? Tell us everything."

Being stoned helped her open up about how she got there, how her parents mostly ignored her, the drive across the country, the dirt she collected, Rachael sending the Oracle in the mail, and her betrayal.

"Skank," Stuart said.

They listened to her troubles with sincere empathy, throwing questions at her for more detailed information.

She talked about her days with Gypsy. How he opened her eyes to the anti-war movement, then vanished like a mirage.

"Douchebag," Sunshine said.

"He had to get back to school. But, being a part of the march today made our time together very valuable."

"If you get a chance, go to a teach-in," Sunshine said, "You'll learn the real facts and issues. The information comes from scholars, not politicians."

"Believe me," Liberty said. "I'm going to find out everything I can. I'm determined to get involved. It was meant to be."

There was no denying Andrea and Sunshine were from families with more money than all the people in North Forks combined. They would never find themselves in her mess, yet they said they admired the courage it took to take off on her own.

It felt restorative to shed the good and the bad, like a baptismal cleansing at the behest of strangers. The conversation flowed easy and natural, making Liberty think she might need friends as much as a place to stay. With that thought, she sat up in a start. "I need to get my car. Everything I own is inside."

"It's three in the morning," Stuart said. "You don't want to go back to your car now.

"I have to."

"Can one of you take her?" Stuart asked.

"I'm too stoned," Andrea said. "It's too late. I'll take her in the morning." She looked at Liberty. "Chill here 'til then."

Liberty woke at noon, still on the beanbag chair, worried. She left the apartment without waking the others.

She had parked Sweet Pea around the corner from the Unicorn, in front of a spinning barber pole on Hayes Street. She headed straight there, fearing vandalism, or worse.

Other than a parking ticket tucked under the windshield wiper, Sweet Pea seemed fine.

"I'm sorry," she said, more to herself than to the car, feeling embarrassed for another foolish decision. "I gotta get it together."

She walked to the *Psychedelic Shop* to check the bulletin board for rooms. "They go fast," the clerk said. "You need to check back every day, maybe twice a day." The people at *The Weed Patch* and the *Trip Without A Ticket* said the same.

Driving up Geary Boulevard, Liberty caught a glimpse of the biggest movie theater she'd ever seen. A sign with the name CORONET shot forty feet up toward the sky. NOW SHOWING, *VALLEY OF THE DOLLS* ran across the marquee.

She stopped at a food store further down Geary to buy the ingredients for Minnesota Hot Dish—the only thing she knew how to make without a recipe.

# 25

Stuart opened the door. "I thought you would wake me up when you went to get your car. Glad you came back. Come on in."

They went into the living room. Andrea and Sunshine were reading magazines and grooving to Simon and Garfunkel's newest album. A guitar accompanied the harmonies as the voices weaved around each other perfectly.

*Tell her to find me an acre of land:*

*Parsley, sage, rosemary and thyme;*

"Were your ears burning?" Sunshine asked. "We've been talking about you."

"I was thinking about you, too. And I'm glad you're home." She plopped down in one of the chairs. "I bought the ingredients to make you dinner as a thank you. They're still in my car."

"And she cooks, too," Sunshine said.

*Between the salt water and the sea strands,*

*Then she'll be a true love of mine.*

"Sunshine and I want you to stay here until you find a place," Andrea said.

Liberty let out a huge breath of relief.

"There's a small room at the end of the hallway past the bathroom. It's more like a big storage closet."

"A storage closet will feel like a mansion after sleeping in my car."

Andrea said, "I called my mom and told her about you. She said it sounds like you could use a break. My parents have an extra mattress we can put on the floor for you. She'll have someone bring it over on Monday. You can use it until you figure out what you're doing."

Liberty put her hands over her heart. "Oh, thank you so much."

"There's only one rule that goes with living here," Andrea said. "It's not our rule, God knows it's not our rule. And it comes directly from my parents, who remind us often, they're paying all the bills."

"What is it?"

"One person per bedroom. No couples. No exceptions. They have made it clear they're not willing to subsidize any freeloading boys. I don't know what's behind it, but they're cool about almost everything else."

"I don't have anyone. I don't even know anyone, except you."

"Well then, it's yours."

At 8:30 Monday morning, Liberty walked the two miles to the main library on Larkin Street. She stood on the sidewalk in front, and marveled at the commanding building and the five oversized sculptures above the front entrance, each perched on a separate pedestal. Carved from stone, they demanded attention and recognition as stoic representatives of Literature, Science, Art, Philosophy, and Law.

A grand staircase led to the main hall on the second floor. Inside, polished oak planks spanned the cavernous space. She found an out-of-the-way table tucked behind a pillar and set her notebook and pen down to claim it.

Her footsteps glided along the massive aisles of hard-bound books containing centuries of wisdom, causing her to remember the pathetic metal building housing the North Forks library.

Through an arched doorway into the vast Periodical Section, she found an area stocked with weekly news magazines. A current event pot of gold going back several years. *Newsweek, Life, Time.*

The first magazine to feature Vietnam on the cover was *Newsweek's* September 21, 1964, issue. The picture on the front was of a man in civilian clothes with his fist over his heart, facing two rows of soldiers. The headline read, "Maxwell Taylor in Vietnam."

After a few hours, dozens of magazines sat open on her table. There were articles about the fear of

Communism and the rationalization of the public's support. She found one article about the White Paper report that stated a need to increase aid to South Vietnam, and another on President Johnson's Operation Rolling Thunder bombing program. They were all justifications for being there, but she couldn't find any articles covering the anti-war movement. Everything she looked at encouraged a thirst for answers, like why the United States went there in 1954 to help the French.

As the day passed, it became clear the media didn't cover the views of the protesters.

The yeasty fragrance of freshly baked bread filled the house on Baker as Liberty climbed the stairs to the apartment. When she opened the door, the smell grew stronger. A tall woman in a gingham half-apron tied around the full skirt of her dress, walked toward her from the kitchen. The woman's thin face and dark eyebrows gave her away as Andrea and Stuart's mother.

"You must be Liberty," she said and reached her hand out.

Liberty shook it. "Yes, hello."

"You have impeccable timing. The bread has about three more minutes in the oven, and then it's ready for us to gobble up."

"I haven't smelled baked bread in a long time. And boy, am I hungry."

"I'm Jackie," the woman said. "And I've heard a lot about you. You have a big fan in Stuart."

Liberty smiled. "He's a great kid."

A sound buzzed from the kitchen. "Finally, it's done. Come with me." Jackie picked up the egg-shaped timer on the counter and twisted it into silence. "Sit down here," she said, nodding toward the small Formica table.

Jackie transferred two plump sourdough loaves to a rack and readied a serrated knife. "Ten minutes, and they should be cool enough.

"Thank you, Mrs." Liberty paused. "I'm sorry, I don't know your last name. Or Andrea and Stuart's."

"Our last name is Sternberg. But please call me Jackie. Just Jackie."

She handed Liberty a plate with two slices of bread smothered in jam and a cup of coffee.

"How'd you spend your day? Sightseeing?"

"No, Mrs...sorry, I mean Jackie. I went to the library."

"The one on Larkin, I hope."

"Yes."

"I love that place. And did you notice how it feels like your feet glide over the floor?"

"Yes. I've never felt it before."

"And it smells like knowledge and emotions." Jackie stopped. "I do get carried away." She looked into Liberty's face like there was nowhere else she'd rather be. "So, tell me. What did you learn in those hallowed halls?"

"I went to study what's going on in Vietnam. It's all people talk about since I've been in San

Francisco." She took a sip of coffee. "It's not like that where I'm from."

"It should be."

"I know a few boys who enlisted and went off to serve because they thought it was patriotic, like people did during World War II and Korea."

"And they most likely signed up to be heroic," Jackie said.

Liberty nodded.

"It's not their fault. They're young and want to be macho."

"People think differently here. That's the reason I want to learn more about this war."

"Conflict," Jackie said quickly and stopped. "Oh, boy, sorry. You just stuck a poker into one of my sore spots." She leaned forward, put her elbows on the table, and clasped her hands. "We, the American people, did not vote for a war. And it fries my ass that the Washington elites think they're cute labeling it a conflict." She was as intense as Gypsy when he had said something similar only three days before.

Jackie leaned against the back of her chair. "Pardon my French, but this mess happened because of our secretive, bizarre little lie that somehow mushroomed into an all-out war." Pure passion oozed from Jackie's every word.

Liberty stored this new tidbit of information with what she had learned at the library.

"There are no perfect politicians, but always remember one thing: the activists are the shining lights of our democracy. They expose the dark corners of government and power."

"Shining Lights." Liberty smiled at the idea.

"I promise I'll get off my soap box," Jackie said. "But not before I say, one more time, the crude warmonger named Johnson has been lying to us every day of his presidency. He single-handedly killed our trust and set in motion this movement."

Liberty shrugged. "Before I got to California, I didn't even know where Vietnam was."

"Sorry, dear. Sometimes, I need to vent. I'm sure you figured out by now, I'm the one encouraging my kids to get involved."

"I can see that."

"If a revolution is taking place in your backyard, you need to engage." Her eyes softened. "Now, enough of my obsession. You were going to tell me what you learned."

"It's confusing. The magazine articles are easier for me to follow than the history books."

"You can't think of this as history. It may have started a decade ago, but it's our current event. The history of this—the truth—will be written later."

"It's hard for me to look at the pictures of the stronger soldiers helping the wounded men to safety."

"Boys," Jackie said. "Imagine yourself being one of those boys in that jungle, and you didn't volunteer to go there."

Liberty shook her head. "So many wounded."

"So many dead." Again, Jackie looked into Liberty's eyes. "If you're serious about learning more, my friend's daughter is involved in a new movement called—I forget. It's got a long name." She laughed. "It'll come to me in a minute. Would you like more bread?"

Liberty nodded.

"The delivery men are scheduled to be here within the hour to drop off your bed. I decided to get you a proper bed."

It was only her second day in the apartment, but she felt more at home than she'd ever been at her parents. Jackie laid another plate of sourdough slices on the table and refilled their cups with coffee.

"That movement I mentioned is called the Spring Mobilization Committee to End the War in Vietnam. For short, they call it Mobe. You can see why." She laughed. "Anyway, it's a new group with big plans for antiwar demonstrations this spring. They aim to involve everyday Americans by informing them what is really going on."

"Your friend's daughter?"

"Her name's Kate Lawson. You should talk to her. She's not much older than you, maybe twenty-one or so, and she's been involved with social justice issues since high school."

Jackie finished the last of her coffee. "She's a scrappy kid. A real go-getter. Smart as a whip." She cleared her throat. "I'll get you in touch with her. You never know, it could turn out to be a front-row seat in a master class on the antiwar movement."

"Mom, you made bread," Andrea yelled. "I smelled it all the way up the stairs."

She rushed into the kitchen, as excited as a ten-year-old. Jackie stood, looking truly happy. She hugged her daughter—a long, precious bear hug. Liberty looked away as her eyes welled at seeing such tenderness given from a mother to her daughter.

# 26

# Harper

# 2020

"Your birthday's coming up," Uncle Kevin said like it hadn't crossed my mind. "The big eighteen. How about we go to The Southern Belly together?"

The thought of me and Mama being there dropped my mood a little. "I don't think I can. Let's pick another place."

"Okay. How about we go to Macon? We can hit the Allman Brothers Band Museum."

"Allman Brothers? Why?

"Because they're the best Southern Rock band of all time."

"In your day, but I'm not feeling it. Megan wants to hang out and celebrate with me."

"Nope. Your birthday's my day—family. Tell Megan she can have the day after."

"Going to Macon's okay, I guess. But let's ditch the Allman Brothers."

He let his disappointment pass. Okay then, I heard about this awesome ghost tour."

"Yes." I pumped my fist.

"And after that, we can go to the Biscuit Barrel." We high-fived.

"Deal."


Uncle Kevin, me, and eight other tour-goers gathered on the corner of Cherry and Fifth, bundled in hooded jackets and winter gloves, waiting for the tour to start at seven.

Our guide arrived on time, dressed like she'd walked off the cover of a Goth rock album, wearing a top hat and velvet cape. Dark makeup circled her eyes.

"Hello, my innocents," she said as she hooked a microphone to her ruffled shirt and handed us wireless earbuds. She asked how many of us had been on a tour before and where we were all from, then suddenly flipped her cape and began.

"I'm Charmaine, your guide. Can everyone hear me?" We all assured her we could.

One of the women asked, "What's your last name?"

"Bellerini. Charmaine Bellerini." She bowed theatrically. "You'll see my name in lights someday, on a Broadway stage. Mark my words." Charmaine bowed a second time.

"Welcome to Macon's most popular ghost tour. Let's get started. Follow me."

We obediently walked behind her as she recited her flamboyant stories of murder, disease, and Macon's haunted history.

Charmaine stopped several blocks down the street and swung her arm out, gesturing like Vanna White. "This is *The Devil's Gate*, our first stop. The elaborate wrought iron masterpiece marks the entrance into this 170-year-old haunted cemetery. When we go inside, I'll point out areas where past disturbances, supernatural aberrations, and bumps in the night have occurred."

Once inside the graveyard about a hundred yards, she jumped on a three-foot retaining wall and, as if it was the Broadway stage she mentioned, she dramatically explained how ghosts are just folks like us, wanting to amuse themselves. She warned, "Stay close together because this is where all the paranormal come out to play."

All that talk of the dead brought Mama to mind. I figured if she was hanging out in a cemetery to amuse herself paranormally on my birthday, it would be with Elvis in the Meditation Garden, singing *Happy, Happy Birthday, Baby.*

Throughout the hour-and-a-half tour, I paid more attention to Charmaine than any of the stories she told. She didn't look much older than me, yet she carried herself with confidence and an enthusiasm for life. She made what could have been a pain-in-the-ass job into a dramatic production. Some people are so easy with life.

One of Liberty's affirmations came to mind. *Turn negative thoughts into positive actions.* I knew they were intended only for her, but that one caused me to want to stop brooding and take a stand about all the things nagging at me.

Pickups and minivans packed The Biscuit Barrel parking lot. "Saturday night busy," Uncle Kevin noted. Couples and families hung out on the front porch rocking chairs like they were rides at an amusement park.

A stone fireplace spanned the far wall of the dining room. We took our place in line behind a black couple in front of the *please wait to be seated* stand.

The hostess returned to the station, looked past the couple and asked Uncle Kevin, "How many?"

"Two."

"This way," she said.

"They was here first," I said.

"I'll get to them in due time. Now, do you want your table?"

"Yes," Uncle Kevin said. "It's her birthday."

She sat us at an oak table for four next to a window overlooking the activity on the front porch.

"I just hate that," I said.

"What?"

Before I could say, the waitress greeted us with glasses of water and plastic menus.

"What do you hate?" he asked when she left.

"It's not right. The way she ignored them and took us first. It's not right."

He looked over to the hostess station and nodded. "They're still there."

"It makes me angry. I feel embarrassed, like I'm better than them. I hate it."

"We're in Macon, Harper. This is *League of the South* country."

"And it's 2020." My voice rose. "It's time something changes."

The waitress returned. Uncle Kevin chose the Grilled Catfish with green beans and mac 'n cheese. I ordered the Chicken Fried Steak with mashed potatoes, carrots, and dumplings.

I'd been tempted to tell him how the diary was fueling my new way of thinking. Still, I thought it best not to, because I'd promised her and Mama I wouldn't share, and I was afraid he might not completely grasp my attachment to it.

"So," I said, channeling her. "I've decided I want my life to have meaning."

"Meaning?" His eyes squinted, and he sat back in his chair. "Listen, I'm no good at reading minds. What kind of meaning are you talking about? Like teaching, or becoming an EMT?"

"Bigger than that."

He raised his eyebrows. "Do tell."

"You know, back in the sixties and seventies, how people marched and protested against the

Vietnam War?" I hadn't thought the conversation through ahead of time.

He laughed. "Good Lord, Harper, where's my niece, and who are you?"

"I'm serious."

"I don't know much about the Vietnam War because it happened at least fifteen years before I was born. And the last time I checked, we're plumb out of anti-war movements."

The waitress set our dinners on the table. After a couple of bites of catfish, he said. "Where'd this Vietnam War stuff come from?"

"Ken Burns."

He looked skeptical. "Since when do you watch documentaries?"

Before my white lie grew into something I couldn't escape, I said, "Come on, Uncle Kevin, I'm serious."

"I know, but jeezus, Harper, you're only one day into your eighteenth year."

"Those kids in Florida, you know, the Parkland School kids? They were younger than I am when they began their fight for gun control."

"Don't tell me you want to take on the NRA?"

"No," I said, exasperated.

"Tell me, what good did those kids really do? Is there a ban on gun shows? No. On online sales? No. Do we have universal background checks? I don't think so."

"At least they tried."

He pointed to my plate. "How's your Chicken Fried Steak?"

"Not bad," I said, but I wouldn't let him distract me. "So, the cause that's been calling to me since I was young, the thing I feel a real connection to and want to get involved in, is Black Lives Matter."

"Black Lives Matter?"

"Yes. Where Deja Washington's working now."

"What happened to her brother was her reason," he said.

"And why shouldn't what happened to her brother be my reason, too? And how about those people who got seated after us because they're black? Their lives matter, too."

He pushed his chin toward me. "And your dumplings? How are they?"

"They're fine," I laughed. "And I feel like Mama would agree. She was always sensitive to injustice."

"I know," he said. "She was tender in that way."

"Remember the bumper sticker she got after they killed Philando Castile?"

"I do."

"I know for sure I need to do more than slap a bumper sticker on my car and wear support buttons. Why are you so against me getting involved?"

"I guess it's just my nature. I suppose I could take my head out of the sand now and again."

"You should try it."

"I was wondering. Do you still have Deja's number?"

# 27

Megan and I went to the Springs Theater every other Thursday for half-off night. We swapped out dinner for two large boxes of Junior Mints and eighty-five-ounce buckets of popcorn.

After the movie, while the credits rolled, we recapped the things we liked—the costumes, the stunts, the makeup. Death scenes and sex scenes rated a thumbs up or down, and the male leads scored 1 to 10. We called ourselves the Forgotten Tomatoes.

For the year after Mama died, except for movie night, I lived the life of a hermit while Megan snuck out at night, exploring the club scene in the towns beyond Hickory Springs.

Since I had just begun the "spreading my wings" phase of my life, she took it upon herself to be my personal social director, scouring the internet for things for us to do.

"Purple Madness has a show this Saturday," she said one day.

"Who's Purple Madness?"

"I haven't seen them, but they're supposed to be great. They're a Prince cover band. The lead singer sounds exactly like him. The band members are all Princed-out, too."

"I've never been to a live concert."

"You're kidding. How did I not know this?"

"You know I haven't. Where is it?"

"Tallahassee."

"I've never been to Tallahassee either."

"Oh, girl, a double dose of firsts. It'll be dope."

"I don't think Uncle Kevin will go for it."

"Excuse me? Didn't you just turn eighteen? Your wings need to fly."

"You know all he's done for me."

"He cares, I get it. But you don't want him to think he can run your life."

I had been too chicken to tell him about our plans until midday on Saturday. His head shook back and forth. "Not a good idea, Harper. I'm responsible for you."

"We'll be fine."

"It's two hours away."

"Megan's a good driver."

"It's not about her driving. Can't you find something to do closer?"

"We already bought the tickets."

"How much?"

"What part of I'm eighteen don't you get?"

He pointed a finger at me but didn't say

anything. He pulled it back. "I'm new at this. Next time, give me more notice."

"I promise."

Easy-peasy. A peck on the cheek and I drove straight to Megan's. We had the place to ourselves. With Prince songs blasting, we brushed purple polish on our nails and experimented with eye shadows. Megan trimmed the front of my hair, giving me what she called "curtain bangs." When done, she pulled out two purple boas from her top drawer.

We drove west on I-35 toward an early sunset. As if we'd ordered it for the occasion, a purple one.

Lights atop twenty-foot poles lit the parking lot next to the club. The concertgoers clumped together in their separate parties, sharing Jello-shots and drugs. We stayed by Megan's car, taking in the surroundings and checking out the craziness. I felt transported to a place where free spirits soared.

A boy with purple streaks in his coarse dark hair walked up to us. His smooth face had high cheekbones and a wide nose. He looked like he could be a relative of Bruno Mars.

"Hi," Megan said.

He wore torn jeans and a bomber jacket over a BLM t-shirt, which piqued my Black Lives Matter fixation. I couldn't take my eyes off him.

"Your hair is fire," he said, looking at me.

I took a huge breath and blinked a couple of times before saying, "Thank you."

He moved closer and playfully nudged me, scanning the parking lot.

"Listen, I can't find my friends. Can I hang with you until they get here?"

"Of course, the more, the merrier," Megan said.

"You girls do weed?"

"Sure." She gave him a big smile and nodded at me.

"Sure," I said, too.

He pulled a joint from his jacket pocket and handed it to Megan.

"You first," she said.

He snapped a lighter and moved it to the joint waiting between his lips. He inhaled and handed it to her.

"Thanks. You give this shit out? Or are you going to charge us?"

"Don't worry about it."

She inhaled and handed it to me.

Libby's first joint had been at the Human Be-In. The parking lot was my turn.

My plan was a timid inhale. When the smoke hit the back of my throat, I bent forward in a coughing fit and handed it back to the boy.

"I was hoping I wouldn't have to admit I never smoked weed before."

"No such luck," he said.

"So, that makes three firsts for the day?" Megan said, proud as all get out.

"Try it again," he said. "Practice makes perfect.

By the way, I'm Mateo."

Relieved by his casualness, I looked into his dark eyes. "I'm Harper."

"You hoo, over here, I'm Megan." She motioned for the joint.

I asked if he put the purple in his hair for this concert. He said, "Yeah, I thought it would add some extra flair."

"That's good shit," Megan said.

He pulled the phone from his pocket to read a text.

"My buddies aren't going to make it."

The three of us went inside together. When Megan showed him our ticket stubs, he said, "Forget those seats. We can do better."

He led us ten rows up the pitched walkway and pointed to three seats in the middle. Megan went in first, and Mateo followed, positioning himself between us.

The pot flowed through my bloodstream. Everything and everyone seemed in harmony. I looked at Mateo's face and honed in on his pouty mouth. He was perfection.

The auditorium went dark as purple lights burst from the ceiling. The band members casually strolled to their places on stage, and the lead singer walked to the center behind a microphone wrapped in feathers.

I was fourteen when Prince died, but to me the man in sunglasses, long purple coat, and a ruffled shirt was the one and only. He began the night with *Raspberry Beret.*

No one at the concert sat. We danced and sang for two-and-a-half hours. My chest pulsed with the music, and happiness washed over me.

On one of the best nights of my life, the three of us left the concert holding hands and singing *Little Red Corvette.* We lingered by Mateo's car. He asked for my number and then called it. I answered my phone.

"Hello."

In stereo, directly in front of me and on my phone, he said, "Hey, now you have my number, too." He hung up. "It was fun hanging out with you."

The drive home was fueled by lightheaded optimism and a steady stream of car lights glistening to and from Tallahassee.

Mama liked to say, "Cities are okay, but coming home is better." Not me. I imagined cities as having heartbeats and personalities, with something to give everyone. Seeing tall buildings jammed together with rows of windows reflecting the sky excited me.

After we crossed the state line back into Georgia, Megan said, "So, you gonna call him?"

My stomach fluttered. "Maybe tomorrow."

"Don't be such a wimp. Call him now."

"He's really cute. His lips. And his hair."

"I think the hair love is mutual."

"Do you think he's been to a Black Lives Matter

protest or just wears the shirt?"

"I don't know. You can ask him when you call him, maybe tomorrow," she mocked.

My phone vibrated.

"It's him," I said and answered.

"Hey, Fire."

I heard loud voices in the background.

"I finally hooked up with my friends. We're at Whataburger on Monroe. Why don't you come hang with us?"

"Ohhh, we're already headed back home."

"Where's home?"

"Hickory Springs, near Tifton."

"Georgia? You live in Georgia?"

"Yes."

"Cool. I thought you were local Tallahassee girls. I live in Nashdale, south of Atlanta."

Someone yelled out his name.

"Our burgers are ready. I'll go past there on my way home next week and text you when I'm close."

It felt like the night had been a dream, like a beautiful blend of music and fun, and then the flutter of eagerness to see him again.

# 28

Four days after the concert, Megan sent me a 911 text about coming to my place when I got off work.

Her car raced up the drive like an ambulance heading to an emergency. She dashed through the door, pulled a paper flyer from the pouch of her sweatshirt, and waived it above her head.

"Look at this. *The Shaky Boots Festival* is May eighth and ninth. We have to go."

"Stop moving it around. I can't read it."

"A Thousand Horses is on the list." She pointed to the scheduled performances. "And Great Peacock. They'll both be there on the same day. And, Colter Wall."

"Your newest obsession," I said.

"You know it. He's got that Johnny Cash vibe, only he's cute."

I snatched the flyer from her hand. "Uncle Kevin's a John Prine fanatic."

"You sure you want him to go? I was thinking it would be more fun if you asked Mateo." She almost smirked.

"He's the only thing I've thought of since he said he'd text me."

"You should have called him."

"I know. It's been four days. It's probably too late now."

"I saw the way he looked at you. He'll call."

We ordered a pizza and talked more about Shaky Boots—whether we should stay over and go both days, what we'd wear, and Mateo.

"Okay, change of subject," Megan said.

"Okay, what?"

"You're going to college, right?"

"Yes. You know I'd be going now if Social Services had their shit together."

"I'm gonna quit," she said.

"What? Why?"

"I know it's only Community College, but the classes are too hard for me. Besides, I've got my mind set on being a tattoo artist and owning a studio."

"What?"

"Yep. For women only."

"Give me a second to process this." I took another piece of pizza from the box. "Tattoo artist makes sense. You've been drawing and doodling all your life. But only for women? Is that a thing?"

"I wasn't sure if it was a cool idea until I did some Googling and found out there really are places like that. Mostly in California."

"Okay, but this isn't California."

"You know how most tattoo places specialize in in-your-face designs? Massive eagles, or skulls, or biker shit?"

I nodded.

"My place will be more like a beauty salon, and I'll serve killer red velvet cupcakes. It'll be like a fun hangout, with no grizzly guys talking about hunting or trying to out-macho each other. Maybe I'll call it *California Style.*"

Megan had clearly been thinking about this for a while. She crunched on the ice cubes in her glass. "I've been working on designs. Ballerina slippers, and butterflies, and flowers. Girl stuff."

She sounded sure and ready. I could imagine her vision, see her salon, and found myself feeling the same twinge of envy I had when watching Charmaine, our tour guide in Macon. Megan was paving her path and visualizing her future. I was still coasting along and losing momentum—a year behind. One of Libby, I mean Liberty's affirmations came alive for me right then. *I choose how I feel.*

"Since I can't enroll until next year," I said, "I still have an itch to get involved with Black Lives Matter."

"I thought that was a phase you were going through."

"No, I'm serious. I even talked to Uncle Kevin about it. But I've been stuck and need help figuring out how to get involved. That's on me."

"You will."

"I read somewhere," I said, not mentioning it was in the diary, "If a revolution is taking place in your backyard, you gotta get involved. It hit home with me. And sometimes when I think about becoming involved, I feel a piece of Mama with me."

"Remind me when the Black Lives Matter thing started."

"Remember the Trayvon Martin killing?"

"Of course. I'm sure everyone in the whole country remembers. We were about ten then."

"And remember the guy who shot him, Zimmerman," I said with disdain. "He said he was scared."

"There's no way he could have been scared of that kid."

"No way."

Megan nodded as my cell pinged.

My heart raced.

"It's him."

The text said *hey fire, cu2mr 6ish lmk where to meet u*

My fingers typed back, *i'll be at work cu@6@ the blue rooster.* I added the address.

My pulse raced as I stood at the hostess station, checking the time, waiting for 6:00 pm. At 6:01 pm, he texted, *traffic stopped still 45 min eta.*

I looked out the double doors every time a set of headlights pulled into the parking lot. He got there at 6:58 pm.

Mateo opened the front door, smiled, and said, "Table for two, please."

I picked up two menus from my station and gave a little curtsey. "This way, sir." My heartbeat sped and I thought about fanning myself with the menu. The woodsy scent of his cologne reached my nose—a smell that would be hard to forget. He settled in the booth I'd picked out, and I sat across from him.

"How have you been, Fire?" His smile seemed sincere, his eyes piercing mine.

"Pretty good." I nodded, keeping my eyes on his, loving the nickname he'd picked for me.

"Do you have to get back to work?"

"No, I can keep an eye on the front door from here."

He sat straight and gave me a thumbs-up.

"How was your time in Tallahassee?"

"Mixed," he said. "On the good side, I met you."

"It was the best part for me, too." I felt a heat move to my cheeks.

Mateo told me about his friend David, who had moved to Tallahassee for a dream job in tech and got laid off after two months. They had grown up together, three houses from each other.

"Kinda like me and Megan," I said. "Is he okay?"

"He was pretty bummed, ya know, feeling like a failure, his dream job gone, and running low on cash."

The way his lips parted, the tip of his tongue showing between them, caused me to forget everything else. I caught myself and looked down at the silverware.

"It's a tough break for someone as smart as him—the top in his class and all that." He paused. "I'm starving. What's good here?"

"You'll never go wrong with the burgers."

"Have one with me?"

"No thanks."

"My treat. Please don't make me eat alone."

"Okay."

After LeRoy took our order, Mateo said, "I missed a week of classes staying in Tallahassee, but it was worth it. David started feeling better, and we got some partying in."

"Where do you go to school?"

"Georgia State."

LeRoy brought the burgers and an extra large basket of fries. He looked at Mateo's shirt.

"I thought all lives mattered," he said, giving me a fatherly, judgmental look before walking away.

"Don't mind him, he's a good guy."

"I'm sure he is, but saying all lives matter isn't cool. It's not cool at all. It's a rude way to shut down conversations about racism."

"He really is a good guy. He's done a lot for me."

"Sorry, it's a pet peeve." He grinned. "Shall we move on?"

"You had on a BLM shirt the other night, too. Do you always wear them?"

He smiled and shrugged. "I wear them a lot. They show the world how I feel." He poured a mound of ketchup on his plate. "The three words, black lives matter, can't be said enough. And the clinched fist reminds me that it's my moral duty to march until the change is made."

The more he talked, the stronger my crush grew. My mind went to when Libby first met Gypsy and how his passion enlightened her on the anti-war efforts, like what Mateo was doing with me. Comparing the similarities between our moments and theirs put me in a light and dreamy place.

"How many of their rallies have you been to?"

"Six or seven. I went to my first one with my mom in 2016."

"With your mom?"

He nodded. "Downtown Atlanta. Hundreds of us marched up Peachtree and then went to the Governor's Mansion for a sit-in. Have you seen it?"

"The Governor's Mansion?" I shook my head. "No. Only pictures."

"I'd never seen a house so big. When I told my mom it looked like something from *Gone with the Wind*, she said, 'That sounds about right because

Nathan Deal's full of hot air.' My mom's nickname for the house is, *The Baloney Bunker*."

I chuckled. "That's funny."

A happiness melted over me as we took turns picking at the fries.

"There's an activist gene in my family," he said. "I've been going to marches since I was in a stroller."

"Wild." I rubbed my arm, trying to imagine a family like that.

"It doesn't even skip a generation. My grandparents have been activists since they met."

"Really?" A sense of awe ran through me.

"For real. When I was a kid, protesting was our weekend jam. Family fun. We'd gather at my grandparents' place, make some signs, and head out to one cause or another."

"What a childhood you must have had."

"I loved it all," he said, grinning. "What kid wouldn't? We danced and banged on drums. We watched people in crazy getups ride unicycles. There were times we'd block off intersections, then the cops would herd us out of the area."

"Wow."

A couple came through the front door. I left to greet them and show them to a window table, then rushed back to Mateo.

When I settled back in the booth, he asked, "What about you? Tell me about your childhood."

"Mine was pretty regular."

Mateo picked up his burger.

"Except I didn't have a dad."

His brow pinched. "No dad?"

I told him how Mama always used to say we were better off, just the two of us. It wasn't my intention, but saying that led to telling him she died. I didn't say how.

"My dad died two and a half years ago," he said. "So I know how hard it is."

I felt my happiness slip and tried to hold off the tears. LeRoy came to our table.

"Is everything okay?"

"Yes, sir, everything's fine," Mateo said.

He looked at me. "You okay, Harper?"

"Thanks, LeRoy. I was talking about Mama, that's all."

LeRoy gave Mateo a pat on the shoulder. "The food's on the house. You might want to change the subject."

A man carrying a briefcase came through the front door. I jumped up and welcome him, thankful for the interruption. He asked for a table where he could spread out his paperwork.

I returned to Mateo. "LeRoy's right. No more sad talk."

"Deal."

"Even though I didn't have a dad, I have an uncle who's better than a dad. I don't know what I'd do without him."

"You didn't have a dad, and I didn't have an uncle." He let out a laugh.

Of all the things I could have asked, despite myself I said, "I'm sorry I keep asking you about Black Lives Matter."

"No problem."

"I've wanted to get involved but don't know how to jump in alone."

"I'll help you."

"That'd be great."

"For starters, get active on the Twitter links. Check out the Campaign Zero website. This movement is ours, and social media is ours. Almost everything you need to know is there.

"And it's important to read the books that will help educate you on the history, so you understand what you're fighting for. Two good ones are *The Warmth of Other Suns*, and *The Color of Law,*" he nodded. "Those will get you started."

"How'd it become so important to you?"

"Like I said, I've spent a lot of time at various rallies. As far as Black Lives Matter, the first protest with my mom was the start, but I was still young. It really kicked in, like, two years ago when I went to the Afropunk Carnival in Atlanta. After that, I was 100 percent. Have you heard of it?"

"No." I grabbed another fry.

"It's rad. It's a weekend music festival with a social conscience. Besides the great music—mostly hip hop and soul—there's art and fashion and ideas, and...It's hard to explain."

My mind imagined being there with him. "It sounds awesome."

"It is."

Mateo said he went because the BLM leaders participated that year, with workshops where local community activists shared firsthand accounts and stories, and global network leaders were there, too.

"I was introduced to people I wouldn't have met anywhere else. Like, Patrisse was leading one of the workshops."

"She's one of the women who started it?"

"Yep, with Alicia Garza and Opal Tometi. They're three badass women. Being in the same space as her motivated me to commit."

I wanted to tell him I know someone who works in the Atlanta office, but wasn't ready to bring up all the Social Services stuff.

He looked at me. "Maybe we can go to next year's Afropunk together."

My smile felt too big. I reached over the table and touched him. I could hardly bear for our time together to end.

"Do you have to get back?"

"Not particularly."

"You want to see my place?"

He pressed his hands to his chest. "Yes."

Our shirts were off before we got to my bed. We explored each other's bodies in a slow, rhythmic manner. I enjoyed a gentleness I'd never experienced before.

"This is nice," he murmured. "I can get used to it."

My heart wanted him.

We texted and FaceTimed every day for two weeks, until he came back to be with me for the weekend.

We wandered hand in hand through the Rhythm and Ribs Festival in Tifton's Fulwood Park. His hand felt soft yet strong, and it heightened my senses. The sky looked extra blue.

The park smelled like a barbeque heaven. Twenty-seven competing teams, under twenty-seven tents, generated clouds of smoke as they prepared to win a piece of the $10,000 prize money.

A rainbow of charming people positioned themselves in front of the booths with big smiles and samples on toothpicks. We chose pulled pork sandwiches from the Butts BBQ team and sweet, soft, homemade whoopee pies from the Chamber of Commerce booth.

Our hips touched as we moved in rhythm with the music playing on the elevated stage at the west end. We were in full dance mode when The Matt Brantley Band came on board.

Never before had I felt so connected when dancing. We were Johnny and Baby. We were

Vincent and Mia without the twist. We danced until they shut down at 10 pm.

After we made love, we sat on my bed with our backs against the wall. I laced my legs through his. He laced his fingers through mine, and we talked.

His hand squeezed mine often when I shared the whole story of losing Mama. It got me through the chain of events from the accident to finding her in the kitchen, without crying. When finished, I felt less heavy.

He drew my face close to his and kissed me. His familiar scent filled me, and I slept straight through the night for the first time in months.

A morning rain shower enhanced my sense of peace. I watched Mateo's back and arm muscles dance as he picked his jeans and t-shirt off the floor and put them on. He sat back on the bed and watched the raindrops caressing the window.

"The drops look like jewels," he said as he reached over and combed my tangled hair with his fingers. He looked into my eyes and whispered, "You're so beautiful."

"And so are you," I said. "Has anybody told you that you look like Bruno Mars?"

He grinned. "I get it a lot. My dad was Filipino, and my mom's white. Bruno's folks were mixed, too."

"How'd your dad die?"

" Thymic carcinoma." He pointed to the top of his chest. "The Thymus gland is about here between the breastbone.

"I'm sorry, Mateo."

He put his arms around me. "It's okay."

"I haven't heard of it before."

"He had a cough for months but hated doctors and didn't see one until it was too late." Mateo sat quietly, then finished. "He fought hard, but Thymic carcinoma won. So, now it's just me and my mom."

"And your grandparents."

# 29

# Liberty

# 1967

Liberty had spoken with Kate Lawson once on the phone. On the second call, she felt comfortable enough to ask questions.

"Jackie said you've been an activist since you were a kid."

"Pretty much my whole life." Kate said. "It comes from a long line of relatives. Mostly my mom. She's spent her life working to make this a better place for her people."

"Her people? What do you mean?"

"The unseen. Hard-working people. Not blue collar; more like grey collar or no collar. She's committed to workers' rights, and fairness. When I was in grade school, our mom made my brothers and me spit swear that we'd say, 'and injustice for none,' when reciting the Pledge of Allegiance at school. It's her motto."

Liberty could see how Jackie was friends with Kate's mother. "She sounds fierce."

"It gets her in trouble. The FBI's always hounding her."

"What for?"

"You name it. It's mostly because she's a Communist, or *was*."

The word hit Liberty like an electric shock. A leper or even a vampire would be more welcome in their house during her childhood.

"I've never known a Communist," she said.

"The word definitely sets off flares. It's synonymous with the boogie man. My mom's not a card-carrying member anymore, but they still track her."

Feeling awkward with the subject, Liberty said, "Tell me about Mobe. I'm not sure I understand the goal."

"I could talk about it all day, but your eyes might start spinning. I'll give you the cliff notes. Mobe's goal is to broaden the peace movement's influence toward ending the war in Vietnam and bring our soldiers home.

"This is so important to me I quit school to join and help organize two of the biggest anti-war marches so far."

She spoke solid and sure. Liberty tried to imagine what the girl on the other end of the phone looked like.

"Marches?"

"One in New York and one here, at Kezar Stadium, on April 15th."

"It's only two months from now."

"And we're finally gaining ground. The ultimate goal is to energize and consolidate all the opposition movements throughout the world."

Overwhelmed by the word world, Liberty took a breath and tried not to sound startled. "Can I help?"

"Meet me at Sparky's in the Castro at 2 pm tomorrow," Kate said. "It's on Church Street. If you get there first, grab a booth."

Liberty hardly slept that night as the hugeness of Mobe's objectives weaved through all the new ways of thinking she'd come across in the past month.

The way Gypsy spoke to her in the Drogstore, and Jackie in the kitchen, and now Kate, felt exciting. All three of them were passionate and committed to a cause, value, or belief, and not afraid to make it known.

Towards morning, energized to do more than simply exist, an ironic thought clipped her conscience. *I have Rachael to thank for all this.* Her world was changing fast.


Liberty used her straw to stab the ice cubes in her water glass and watched an assortment of the city's finest eccentrics move about Sparky's as though playing a game of musical chairs.

Conversations buzzed. People arrived and left in waves. A young woman in jeans and an unbuttoned pea coat opened the front door. She yelled, "Give me Liberty."

All eyes turned her way. Liberty shot her arm in the air.

"Here."

Kate was no more than five feet tall. Her dark hair and thick eyebrows overpowered her soft, light skin. She moved toward Liberty with a sure stride. A leather bag hung from one of her shoulders, and an overstuffed tote with a peace sign appliqué from the other.

"Sorry, I'm late. My last errand took longer than expected, but well worth it."

A cloud gently eased past, sending a beam of light through the window as Kate plunked the tote on the table, took off her coat, and scooched over the padded seat across from Liberty. Her schoolgirl face was at odds with the robust, confident sound of her voice.

"Look, look at these," she said and reached inside the bag. "Fresh off the press." She tossed two campaign pins across to Liberty. The yellow one had black lettering. It read, *End The War In Vietnam NOW.* The other, *Mobilization To End The War In Vietnam Now, April 15,* was green with blue print.

Every inch of Kate's face beamed. "You're the first person to see these other than the printer and me. They're why I'm late. Aren't they groovy?"

Liberty picked up the green pin. "Sure are."

"People will be wearing these both here and in New York. Put it on."

A waitress came to the table. "I'm Darlene. What can I get you?"

"Just coffee. Two cups," Kate said.

Liberty released the back of the pin in her hand and slid it easily through her blouse.

"Perfect," Kate said. "Now you're one of us."

Kate pulled a stack of flyers from the leather bag and handed half of them to Liberty. "Would you mind folding these in thirds while we talk."

Darlene brought their coffee to the table. "Refills are free here." Kate leaned in and lowered her voice. "Something happened yesterday, and I'm just about to bust out of my skin."

"What?" Liberty said while folding her second flyer.

Sounding confidential, Kate said, "Martin Luther King asked James Bevel to get involved with Mobe, as the National Director. Yesterday he accepted."

Liberty knew who Martin Luther King was but never heard of the other guy.

"As if that wasn't good enough, this morning we learned King agreed to speak at the New York rally." Kate slapped the table four times. "This is huge. It's going to make all the difference." She sat back and raised her fist. "The Reverend James Luther Bevel. Hallelujah."

"Fantastic."

She looked at Kate, poised like a warrior, a woman of action, and asked, "How old are you?"

"Twenty-one."

Liberty shook her head. "You told me about your mom, but how did you get here, doing this?"

"In high school, my friends and I were more interested in current events than sports or being popular. Marta's parents had a portable Zenith in their living room and whenever we could, we watched The Big News on Channel 5.

"When we saw the coverage of the sit-ins in Tennessee and North Carolina there was no stopping us. To see those protesters, just a little older than us, got us started. They were our heroes."

Liberty thought, *that's one more thing I have to learn about.*

"We were idealistic as hell and inspired, you know?"

Liberty looked up from her flyers and nodded.

"So, Marta and I started a club to fight our high school's Sororities and Fraternities over their segregated table setup in the quad. It was our quad, too, and we were being discriminated against by not being allowed to sit at their tables."

Liberty studied Kate in awe.

"We came up with the name *The Freedom Righters.*"

"The Freedom Righters," Liberty repeated and smiled.

"They didn't take kindly to us crashing their tables, but the school sided with us."

"How old were you?"

"Fourteen or fifteen. It felt really good to win. From there, we moved on to the real work." Kate took a breath. "Outside of school, you know?"

Liberty saw a light in Kate's eyes, a serene confidence.

"Like what?"

"We got word the Cal students were boycotting the Woolworth in Berkeley, and four of us took the bus there to join them. We were the youngest, and not five minutes after we got there, they hauled us off to jail."

"Good Lord," Liberty said. "Really?"

"More than once. We were only held until our parents came to pick us up. My mom couldn't have been prouder."

They folded flyers and spoke for over two hours. Kate did most of the talking. It was clear she had steered her own destiny.

While learning more about Kate, Liberty slipped into the comparison game. The only thing she'd done well was land a job at Dairy Queen and perfect the swirl. She closed her eyes and thought, *My life will have meaning.*

"I'm here for you."

"Welcome aboard. Jackie told me how you left home and drove out here alone. That took guts. The kind of guts I need."

Kate stopped folding the flyers and sat tall. "One more thing I need to tell you. Yesterday, they named me the Executive Director of the West Coast rally."

"At Kezar?"

"Yes, and I'd like you to be my assistant."

"Whatever you need."

"I've known Jackie since I was ten. Her word is all I need." She looked at her watch. "Shit. I gotta go."

She left her folded flyers on the table. "Can you hand these out before you leave?"

Giddy with excitement, Liberty said, "Sure."

As Kate hitched her bags on her shoulders to leave, she said, "I'm sure Jackie told you we don't get paid for this work. At least not yet."

She lifted her right hand and gave Liberty the peace sign.

# 30

The talk with Kate swirled through Liberty's head as she stood on the sidewalk in front of Sparky's, handing flyers to passersby unaware of what she had just learned.

Had it been real? Kate said his name, Martin Luther King Jr., like he was an everyday man, accessible to her. Trusting the reality of being part of something as massive as Kate had explained would take time.

When the last flyer had been handed out, she drove straight to the library on Lawson to soak up everything they had on James Bevel.

Kate had mentioned the Freedom Riders two hours earlier. Ironically, during her research she learned Bevel and his wife helped recruit the volunteers and rode on the first bus with them.

She found out that from the birth of the SNCC, to the Selma to Montgomery march, Bevel was at

King's side. If nothing else, she learned the man was determined to make a change.


Andrea sat at the kitchen table studying physics, her dark hair pulled back in a bun.

"You look scholarly," Liberty said.

"Hi, Lib. Man, physics is a drag." She set her glasses on the table and rubbed her eyes. "It's a good time for a break. Coffee?"

"I'll get it." Liberty filled two mugs with the last of the coffee in the pot.

"Kate Lawson phoned about an hour ago. She wants you to call her back." Andrea narrowed her eyes to read the pin on Liberty's blouse. "Was today the day you met with her?"

"Yes," Liberty gushed. "Yes." She looked at the veneer cabinets and yellow Formica countertops as her head overflowed with the twists and turns that took place to bring her there. She told Andrea about their meeting and the James Bevel news.

"Whoa." Andrea set her cup down. "So, you'll meet him?"

Liberty nodded, unsure. "I'm embarrassed to say I never heard of him until today. How do you know about him?"

"You don't grow up with parents like mine and not know about all the players in the Civil Rights Movement."

"Maybe I'm in over my head."

"You're smart. You'll figure it out. The one thing I know for sure is if you're serious about getting involved, you've got to give it a hundred percent." Andrea plucked the receiver from the wall phone. "I gotta call my mom and tell her about your Bevel news."

"Wait, I didn't tell you the best part. Martin Luther King Jr. is going to speak at the New York demonstration."

"She's going to freak out. First-hand news."

When Andrea hung up, Liberty called Kate, who asked her to pick up five boxes of flyers from the printer and have them folded by Friday morning. She gave her an address for the print shop and a second address in Berkeley. "Be there with the flyers on Friday at noon for a steering committee meeting."

After four hours of folding, Liberty's hands needed a break, and her bankroll needed a paying job. She set out on foot, ignoring the pot shops, liquor stores, and beauty salons, figuring she'd be more suited for waitressing or selling clothes. Seven places didn't need help, and two had her fill out applications.

On the corner of 10th and Mission, a huge fiberglass dog head rotated on a ten-foot pole high above the roof of a diner. The dog, a dachshund, wore a white chef's hat and a blue polka-dot bow tie. A *Help Wanted, Part-Time* sign hung in the window of The Doggie Diner.

Liberty sat on one of the red stools at the stainless steel counter. A man with pale rows of scalp showing through his thin hair came over. He could have been around thirty-five, or fifty. His nametag said Larry, and underneath, Manager.

"What can I get for you?"

"I saw your sign, and I need a job."

"Whow," Larry said. "A new record. It hasn't been there for more than ten minutes. Let's sit at one of the corner tables and have a talk."

When they settled in, Larry said, "I hear a little Minnesotan in your accent."

"North Forks," she replied.

"Iron range country."

"You know it?"

"Spent my first thirty years in the land of ten thousand lakes." He smiled. "Up by Park Rapids, to be exact."

She told him about her job at the Dairy Queen. As luck would have it, Larry worked at a Dairy Queen, too, one summer when he was a kid. That's all it took.

"I'll give you a try," he said. "Us Minnesotans got to stick together. Fill out this application while I take the sign out of the window."

Twenty minutes later, she walked out of The Doggie Diner as a part-time employee working the evening shift on Tuesdays and Thursdays.

# 31

Liberty found a parking place two blocks from the address in Berkeley. Carrying the boxes of flyers, she walked down Telegraph Avenue past exotic smells from ethnic restaurants. Under the blue and white striped awning above the sidewalk in front of Caffe Mediterraneum, she found the street number, 2475.

The bittersweet tang of roasted coffee and cigarette smoke dominated the place. She scanned the packed room for Kate, then asked the man behind the long coffee bar if he knew her.

"She's up there," he said, pointing to a stairway to the mezzanine. Liberty hesitated before climbing the steps.

Toward the back wall, Kate and five men sat at a rectangular table strewn with papers and coffee cups.

"Hi, Liberty," Kate said. "Come have a seat. I'll introduce you."

She placed the boxes on a side table and hung her coat over the back of an open chair.

"Everyone, this is Liberty. I brought her on board to be my assistant."

"Assistant?" one of the men said. "What the fuck. Who has an assistant?"

Kate looked at the others and laughed. "Gentlemen, let this day go down in history. Jerry Rubin found a word that offends him." She looked back at Jerry. "How about helper? Better? Supporter? I need help, and she's here to do that."

Jerry held up his hand. "Touché, Lawson, carry on."

"Don't mind him, " Kate said to Liberty. "He's always like this."

"And proud of it."

A beaded headband cut through the middle of his forehead under wild, curly hair. Pinned to his shirt, a pink campaign button with red lettering said, *Vote Jerry Rubin Mayor/A New Community.*

She remembered seeing him hop on the stage at the Be-In when the Grateful Dead took a break.

"Were you at the Be-In?"

"Damn straight," he said. "Running for Mayor's a full-time job."

She was with Gypsy and hadn't listened to what he said.

"And this is Bernie," Kate continued. "He's our master leafleteer. He'll be taking those boxes off your hands."

Bernie raised his eyebrows as if to say hi. Bald with a gray beard, he looked to be the oldest man in the room—maybe in his sixties.

"And Fred," she continued. "He keeps things on track and helps us stay out of trouble."

Fred, a giant of a man, nodded impatiently. "Tim counts our beans. Abby's our secret weapon with publicity, and you already met Jerry."

Fred said, "Okay, let's get started. I assume everybody here knows about Bevel coming on board?" Liberty joined the others with nods all around. "We caught ourselves a big fish."

Fred cleared his throat. "I've been working on finalizing our official call for the demonstration. He handed copies of his draft to everyone. "Scribble down your thoughts as we go. There will be a shit pile more drafts, but we'll open with something like this." His voice boomed as big as he was.

"We call all Americans to unite and mobilize in a movement to end the senseless slaughter of our GIs and the mass murder of the Vietnamese people."

Overwhelmed with the seriousness of his words, Liberty crossed her arms and looked at the floor. Its checkerboard pattern sent her mind to the terrifying moment when Alice tumbled down the rabbit hole into a place stranger than reality. A place she didn't belong. He continued reading. "As the war cruelly destroys in Vietnam..."

Liberty studied each face at the table, all committed, forceful, and serious. She was among a handful of critical players who were there to make it happen. It crossed her mind that everything of consequence starts with a small group sitting around a table like this. She imagined the founding fathers drafting the Declaration of Independence.

Fred ran his finger under the words and bobbed his head with each new sentence. They painted a vivid picture of what Mobe intended to achieve. He finished with, "We declare not merely a protest but a new beginning."

"Fuck yeah," Jerry said. "But it needs to be more radical. It sounds like something my Zaydee wrote. We need more passion. Grab 'em by the balls, and don't look back."

"Okay, Jerry," Fred said with little conviction. "I'll make a note of it."

As the meeting went on, the strategic planning discussions grew louder, with shouting matches between Jerry and Tim and then Fred and Abby. It took a while before Liberty recognized the sparring that took place was necessary for each member to get to the same conclusion.

Bernie rapped on the table with his U.S. Army Zippo lighter, to get their attention.

"Change of subject. We need to bypass the media." he said. "Since it's those fucker's policy to stonewall covering our demonstrations, we'll have to expand the hand-outs and mailings."

"We need to raise money to do that," Kate said.

"Not exactly a can of worms, but close."

"Let's try to fundraise at the same time," Kate said. "We can put a coupon for contributions on everything we hand out."

"Two birds," Bernie said. "Good thinking. I'll get my team to smother the towns from South Bay to North Bay with our propaganda, and I'll get Don on board to rally the vets."

"Duncan?" Abby asked.

Bernie nodded and looked at Liberty. "He's working with the VVAW. The Vietnam Veterans Against The War. And active duty GIs, too." He added, "If you haven't read his article in this month's *Ramparts*, do it." He tapped his lighter on the table again. "It rips the war efforts a new asshole."

Fred jumped in. "It sounds like you've got a good plan. We're falling behind on our volunteer efforts, though. We need to double the numbers. Liberty, do you want to take that on?"

She froze. *In another moment, down went Alice after the White Rabbit, never once considering how in the world she was to get out again.* Her stomach cramped. She said, "Yes."

"Make sure you organize them around what they can do," Abby said. "And more importantly, what they want to do. It's the key to success."

"We've got work to do," Fred said. "Let's wrap this up and circle back here or at Jerry's pad next Wednesday."

"My place is cool," Jerry said.

Liberty picked up the draft of the final call for the demonstration Fred had placed in front of her. "Can I take this with me?"

"Of course," Kate said. "And I'll get you the existing volunteer contacts by the end of the week. You can build from there."

# 32

Liberty, Jerry, and Kate walked down the stairs together.

"I know you probably think you're green and in over your head," Kate said. "We all were once, and look at us now—kickin' ass."

"I was born kickin' ass," Jerry said as they crossed through the cafe.

"Liberty?" a voice called.

She turned to see Gypsy in his fringed jacket and necklace of arrowheads, standing behind a table. A burst of confusion, anger, and a flashback of his van driving away set off a dizzy spell. He walked toward her.

"Later," Jerry said and left.

Gypsy came close and wrapped his arms around her. She stiffened and backed away from him.

"What are you doing here?"

"I came back to look for you."

"What?"

"I couldn't stop thinking about you. You've been

on my mind every day since I left. Leaving with no way to contact each other was the most idiotic thing I've ever done."

Kate cleared her throat. "Are you cool with this? Do you want me to stay?"

"No, it's cool."

"Okay, then I gotta run." She gave a wave. "I'll get that list to you."

Liberty flinched when Gypsy touched her arm.

"I'm sorry. I'm so, so sorry. Come to the table and sit with me."

"No. Not until you tell me how you knew I'd be here."

"I didn't. This is some kind of karma, or kismet, or miracle."

She shook her head. "What are you talking about? This feels weird. Why are you doing this?"

"I had to find you."

"I'm confused. Why are you at *this* place looking for me? I've never been here before."

"It's famous. Alan Ginsberg used to be a regular. Before heading to the city to look for you, I stopped here for lunch on the off-chance I might get to see him." He shrugged. "I gave myself three days to look for you, and if I couldn't find you, I planned to drive to North Forks. You and me here at the same time is a million-to-one stroke of luck."

Being so close to him again set off an outbreak of sensations. Gypsy took her hand. "Let's sit down."

She followed him to his table.

"Do you want anything?"

"No."

Gypsy breathed in. "It's my turn to be confused. I told you why I'm here. So, what are you doing here? And, was that Jerry Rubin?"

"Yes. Do you know him?"

"I know who he is. Everyone knows who he is. But how do you know him?"

"I only met him today. And Abby Hoffman, and Fred Halstead."

Gypsy looked stunned.

"And Bernie someone, and Tim someone. I forgot their last names."

"What?" he said. "I mean, WHAT?"

"I'm working with Mobe."

"How?"

"Pretty wild, huh? It's a long story."

His voice rose. "It's barely been a month since I left."

"It's been a month exactly," she said.

"I know. I'm sorry. Tell me how you got involved with Mobe."

"You started it all," she said. "Remember the last day we were in the Drogstore?"

"Of course. January 19th. Stupid Idiot Day."

She laughed. "You quoted Steinbeck to me."

"What do I believe in? What must I fight for, and what must I fight against?"

"Yes. I couldn't shake the words. It upset me that I had never believed in anything."

He kept his eyes on her as he drank his coffee.

"You talked with such passion it lit a spark inside me. It turned into flames, and I needed to learn what was going on."

She told him about meeting Stuart at the march, and how living with Andrea and Sunshine was the first time she felt like a part of a family—accepted for herself.

And Jackie, who had become her north star. "I've never met anyone like her before. She's kind and smart and everything I'd want to be."

She heard herself talking too much, but there was more to say—about meeting Kate and being invited to get involved, and how out of place she felt in the meeting upstairs.

Gypsy smiled. "I'm so proud of you."

"Sorry, Chatty Cathy, here. I should have asked about you. What have you been doing? How are the teach-ins going at school?"

"Going good. There are over 70 locations across the country now. I've been coordinating with their local radio stations to record and broadcast the meetings."

"What a great idea."

Liberty didn't know if the unlikely chance to see him again was a coincidence or fate, but she did know she wanted to be with him.

Gypsy followed her back to the apartment to meet Andrea and Sunshine. Finding they were alone, she took his hand and led him to her tiny room. They

Page 216

quickly undressed. His rapid heartbeat heightened the intense passion that had not faded from their times before.

When they surfaced from her room, Andrea and Sunshine were in the kitchen, grilling bologna sandwiches. Andrea frowned when they entered. "Who's this?"

"This is Gypsy," Liberty said.

Andrea flipped the sandwiches. "We've heard all about you," she said with an edge. "You took off without a word. Not cool."

"I know. I made a big mistake. That's why I came back."

"You can't treat someone in love with you like that."

"I know. I acted like a douche."

"I agree. Have a seat," Andrea said. She handed both of them a mug of coffee.

"Nice place," Gypsy said.

"Thanks. I hope you're not planning on staying here."

"Um, no."

"Good."

"What's going on?" Liberty asked.

Andrea's anger shifted to her. "The day you moved in, we told you about my parent's only rule."

Sunshine said to Gypsy, "No couples can live here. Andrea's parents pay the bills, and they draw the line with the number of people they support."

"You just took one hell of a leap Why would I

want to live here when I have my own place?"

"I told you about his van," Liberty said. "The apartment was empty and we took advantage of a little alone time."

When Andrea and Sunshine finally left for their evening class, Gypsy said, "Listen, Lib, how about we live in the van for a few months? I know it's funky, but the price is right, and we can be together. The truth is, I wouldn't want to live here even if there weren't any rules."

"What about Portland, and school, and SDS?"

He ran his finger down her nose. I'm going to enroll at SFSU, and SDS has an office here on Howard Street."

"Do your parents know about this?"

"They're not happy about it, but I am." He smiled. "I know it's crazy, but we can make it work."

A bubble of certainty traveled through her spine. "Well, what are we waiting for?"

Gypsy hugged her. "Together, we'll change the world.

# 33

# Harper

# 2020

On Thursday, April 2nd, five weeks before Megan and I planned to go to the Shaky Boots Concert, I drove home on my lunch break to watch Judge Judy. I liked to scour the gallery for the lady I had named Wanda. She sat in the audience section wearing a disguise almost every show, but her dark, angry eyebrows gave her away.

Instead of Judge Judy on the bench, news anchors sat behind a desk with a *Breaking News* ribbon across the bottom of the screen. In a small box to the side, a live feed camera focused on a lectern in front of the Georgia State Capital. Not thirty seconds had passed before Governor Kemp walked up to the stand.

I still had the remote in my hand, so I switched the channel. Governor Kemp was on that channel, too.

"Good afternoon, everyone," he said. "Today I'm joined by Lieutenant Governor Geoff Duncan..."

I switched the channel again, only to see the same thing. "As of noon today, we now have 18,947 COVID-19 cases in Georgia with 733 deaths."

I hadn't concerned myself with COVID-19. It was something that started in China and spread to New York, so hearing it had made its way to Georgia was a surprise to me.

"We understand that these are more than just numbers," he said. "These are Georgians."

A bearded man dressed like a preacher stood on the steps behind the governor. He bobbed and weaved, and his fingers fluttered.

I'd only seen people sign with their hands, but his whole body danced with expression and energy as he explained Kemp's bleak message to the hearing impaired. I had a hard time taking my eyes off him.

"Tomorrow, I will sign a shelter-in-place order for all Georgians, with an expiration date of April 30th."

"What?" I yelled at the television. "What are you talking about? A month?" I slumped forward, trying to figure out how a person, let alone a whole state, could stay home.

"I am confident that together we will emerge victorious from this war. With help and God's grace, we will build a safer, stronger, and more prosperous state for our families and generations to come. Thank you, and God Bless."

"A more prosperous state?" I yelled at the screen again. "How can staying home make us more prosperous?"

When I called the hardware store, the manager said, "Stay home. We'll figure this out and let you know."

I called Megan. "Did you see this shelter-in-place speech?"

"No, I'm working on my designs. What speech? What does shelter-in-place mean?"

"Means you can't leave your house." I gave her a couple of the bullet points.

"Does it mean, like, my mom can't do hair?"

"I guess. Not until April 30th."

"That's an eternity," she said. "But we can still go to Shaky Boots, right? It's not until May."

"There's no way this crud can last that long. No way."

I called Mateo.

"Kemp's overreacting," he said. "He's covering his ass. If he doesn't make a big deal, it'll look like he doesn't care. No politician wants that." He laughed. "My mom yelled at the television throughout the whole speech. She's not a fan."

"I did, too," I laughed. "I want to meet her."

"You will."

The Blue Rooster and the hardware store shut down until further notice. I sheltered in place, getting more worried each day. Kemp had said 733

Georgians died. More than a fourth of the people who live in Hickory Springs.

My news app began to announce the death totals by regions and highlight the grand total in a box on the lower left side of the screen.

I drew squares on a sheet of paper, dated them to April 30, and scotch-taped it to the wall by the front door. First thing in the morning, after checking the numbers, I wrote the death toll on its designated square.

And, even though I'd never been there, and New York City was a thousand miles from Hickory Springs, I faithfully watched Governor Cuomo's daily press conference, keeping my eyes on the refrigerated trucks with the leftover dead bodies parked behind the hospitals. Thinking about the people who had been rolled out of the hospital in bags and stored inside those trucks messed with my head.

After three weeks, the President of the United States said he thought we should hit our bodies with a tremendous amount of ultraviolet light through our skin or some other way. It didn't seem right.

The numbers, and deaths, and warnings pulled me down. Trying to shake off my funk, I found a blog with 100 things to do while in quarantine.

Some suggestions were plain old stupid, like learning pig Latin and practicing writing with your non-dominant hand. Some, not so stupid, like looking at pictures of puppies and watching films that won Best Picture at the Oscars.

Number seventeen caught my eye. Plant a home garden. Mama didn't have much of a green thumb, so the only gardening I'd done was to poke toothpicks into sweet potatoes and balance them on the rim of glass jars filled with water.

Without consulting Charlotte, I decided she'd like a bed of homegrown vegetables moving into the space next to her, and I ordered some seed packets online.

After finding a shovel, a hoe, and a couple of large screwdrivers in Uncle Kevin's tool shed, I quickly learned turning over rock-hard soil took more strength than I had. Uncle Kevin came to the rescue. He called it tilling.

I planted and watered, and waited for the seeds to sprout. The smell of damp soil became part of my day. The waiting gave me a scrap of hope that good things would come. Whoever said gardening can soothe a troubled mind wasn't kidding.

Uncle Kevin spent the better part of April working overtime due to the explosion of online shopping and medicine deliveries. When things turned less chaotic, he helped me expand the garden with Red Leaf and Romaine, then radishes and zucchini. He built a butterbean tent to create height.

For our tomatoes, we chose two varieties—big, solid Beefsteaks and long, skinny San Marzanos. We added basil and thyme plants to repel the whiteflies and aphids.

The sweat of hard work and the smell of the

earth eased my fears and calmed my death toll obsession.

# 34

It became clear Governor Kemp and all the other know-it-alls were wrong about the pandemic going away when the weather warmed up. It had swooped in like a doomsday cloud hovering over the whole world, with no desire to leave. Hand washing and six-foot distancing didn't seem to slow the death totals or the bombardment of frightening information.

I made another hand-drawn calendar and taped it over the first one. The U.S. death count on May 1, was 63,023.

While I stayed put at home, Mateo and his mother dressed in full protective gear—disposable coveralls, gloves, masks, and goggles. They handed out donated groceries to people who drove to the food bank facility and waited in lines circling the block.

I'd never known anyone as brave and kindhearted as him. I was not brave. He started calling me Little Miss Covid Crazy.

I spent most of my mornings pampering the

vegetables under Charlottes watchful eye, then gave myself an afternoon escape with a movie. *Clueless, Inside Out, Sisterhood of the Traveling Pants, Juno.*

One day, after watching *Notting Hill*, I turned to The Dr. Bill Show, our regional Dr. Phil copycat. Dr. Bill leaned forward from a tall chair with his arms crossed. He spoke to the woman across from him like he thought he was the almighty judge of her life. The camera went in for a close-up of the watery grey mascara stains running down her cheeks.

"It's time to stop complaining, making excuses, and pointing fingers," he said as he pointed his finger at her. "Stop thinking of yourself as a victim."

It reminded me of how Eddie used to talk to me. In a flash of anger, I aimed the remote at his egg-shaped head, pointed it toward the middle of his forehead, and pressed the button. The screen went black.

I couldn't get that woman's face out of my mind. She went to the wrong show for help, only to be humiliated. Then I thought of how Mama went to a doctor who didn't give a damn. And how Deja Washington's brother drove past the wrong cops. Killer cops.

Still, Dr Bill's advice came back to me. *It's time to stop complaining and making excuses.* His words could have been said about me. COVID-19 had chipped away at my ability to make plans and dreams about the future. I had fallen in love and blamed the pandemic for keeping us apart.

I turned the television back on. The Dr. Bill show had been interrupted for a breaking news announcement. The newscaster spoke with clipped urgency. "Just in, newly released video of the fatal shooting of a black jogger over two months ago, back on February 23rd. A warning. What we're about to show you is disturbing."

He spoke over a video showing a black guy jogging down the road of a neighborhood lined with moss-covered oaks. It had been recorded on the cell phone of a man following him in a truck.

Further up the street, a white 4 x 4 pickup blocked the jogger's path. A white man pointed a shotgun at him from the truck bed, and the driver's door was open. I walked to the television and stood in front of it, my pulse racing.

The jogger maneuvered to get around the truck. The driver jumped out of the cab with a shotgun. The jogger went toward him, and the man fired directly into his chest. The jogger stumbled a few steps and fell across the yellow line on the road. The shooter remained over the lifeless man with his weapon still pointed at him.

The newscaster said, "Gregory McMichael and his son Travis McMichael are still free men this morning, with no charges filed against them. According to the police report, they were trying to make a citizen's arrest and shot twenty-five-year-old Ahmaud Aubrey in self-defense. Gregory McMichael is a former cop."

A banner on the bottom of the TV said, AHMAUD ARBERY SHOOTING IN GEORGIA /WSB TV.

My heart rushed. My head pounded. I couldn't shake the cold-bloodedness of what I'd seen, and the way those men acted like they were out for a casual day of hunting.

I pushed the rewind button to watch it again.

*And what if Ahmaud Arbery hadn't jogged down the wrong road? Or if the McMichael's had stayed home that day?*

I called Mateo.

"Hey, Fire."

"Have you seen the video?"

"I just saw it on Twitter."

"Is there going to be a protest?"

"I haven't seen anything organized so far. You thinking about leaving your house?" he teased.

"Believe it or not, yes."

The next day, a hundred protesters came together in the town of Brunswick. With fists raised and gazes firm, I watched on my phone as they marched down the very street where Ahmaud died, demanding justice.

Seeing those committed and unafraid activists magnified my shame about being a coward. Not even the pandemic discouraged them. Liberty had said in her diary. *I can feel fear and move forward at the same time.*

# 35

# Liberty

# 1967

A few days before the meeting at Jerry Rubin's apartment, Gypsy asked Liberty if there was any way he could sit in.

"I don't know. They weren't too friendly toward me the last time. Especially Jerry, but I'll tell Kate how involved you are with SDS and see what she thinks."

They drove to the meeting in nervous silence. Gypsy maneuvered the rain-soaked streets while Liberty concentrated on the rhythm of the windshield wipers, commanding herself to be more than an observer this time. Jerry lived at the corner of Dwight and Telegraph, a block from Caffe Mediterraneum.

"Here goes everything," Gypsy said as they approached the front door. Jerry greeted them with a nod. He shook Gypsy's hand. "Hey man, Kate briefed us on your work with SDS. Enter freely and of your own will."

Gypsy replied, "Nice Bram Stoker reference."

Several people were seated at the dining table. Liberty glanced into the living room. Psychedelic posters covered the walls. Stacked boxes of flyers and hand-outs that politicians might need dominated the middle of the room. Contrary to Jerry's personality, it all appeared organized.

In addition to the people at the last meeting, there were three new faces. After Liberty and Gypsy introduced themselves, the man to the right of Gypsy said, "I'm Ed Keating, Vice Chair of Mobe."

The man next to Keating said, "I'm Paul Heide with the ILWU, Local 6."

"Don Duncan here," the third man said.

After Bernie had mentioned Don Duncan's article at the last meeting, Liberty read it. She studied the lines on Duncan's forehead and could hardly look away.

Keating said, "If you don't know, we got unanimous support from the Longshoremen leaders this week, thanks to Paul."

"Man, that's a huge step forward," Jerry said. He pulled a cigarette pack from his pocket. "The unions have made a hell of a difference. People are coming out of the woodwork and won't be silenced." He tapped out a cigarette. "We'll show Washington we're Goddamned united." Jerry lit his cigarette. "This is fuckin' inspirational. The power is in our hands. Power to the people."

"I agree," Keating said. "What's going on with the volunteer efforts?"

Nervous but ready, Liberty leaned in, hoping they'd take her seriously.

"I took Abby's advice about organizing them by what they want to do."

"Smart," Abby said."

"I found a trash can filled with data-processing punch cards, and scooped up all of them."

"Punch cards?" Keating asked.

"Yes, I used them to rig up a system to match the volunteers with their interests. There's a card for each volunteer," she said. "Different holes on the cards represent a task. One for people who speak Spanish. Another for those who want office work. Others to organize or go door-to-door. I match the recruit's choices to the various holes."

"I'd like to see how it works," Abby said.

"If we need people to hang flyers or stand on street corners handing them out, I push a knitting needle through the related holes in the stack of cards and lift. Those people are identified and the phone duty team makes the contacts."

"Genius," Keating said.

Liberty's breath caught as the word rushed past her ears. *Genius.* One small word that had never passed her way before. Gypsy patted her on the shoulder.

"Our numbers are growing each day," she said.

"Sounds good. Let's move on to the event," Keating said. "Speakers? Who have we confirmed so far?"

"Coretta Scott King has finally agreed," Kate said. "She'll be here while her husband speaks in New York. Plus, we've got Julian Bond and Eldridge Cleaver on the schedule."

"Couldn't ask for better. Great job."

The names swirled in Liberty's head. Leaders and uniters from across the country, signing up to help the cause. To be in a place where their names were spoken would have not been possible a month before.

"And, drum roll, please," Kate added. "Judy Collins, Big Brother, and Country Joe all said they'd perform."

Keating nodded. "It's crunch time. Let's move on to the venue."

Bernie opened a set of drawings on the table. "Sam couldn't make it, but he sent these plans noting places of vulnerability and prospective problems or concerns.

After studying them, and discussing logistics and security, the meeting began to wind down. Gypsy said, "I'll get with the top people at SDS and coordinate their mobilization. They're ready."

"Sounds good. You came at the right time," Keating said, checking his watch. "Six weeks will go by quick. Let's rally back here next week to check boxes and tie up loose ends. Same time."

Keating's praise helped her confidence. Each day, more volunteers came on board, anxious and ready to do whatever it took. Her squad informed her of the locations and times of the many marches and peace rallies spread through the area.

On the weekends, she and Gypsy packed the van with leaflets, buttons, and people, traversing the city, mingling with marchers, soliciting people to join, and spreading the word about the demonstration opposing the war. Andrea, Sunshine, and Stuart were her top lieutenants.

On April 4th, eleven days before the fifteenth, Martin Luther King, Jr. delivered a speech in New York City denouncing America's involvement in the war. He opened with the line, "A time comes when silence is betrayal." The next day, support for Mobe mushroomed throughout the country.

Each morning, as they drank coffee in the van and discussed the accomplishments of the prior day, Liberty jotted them down in her diary.

On the evenings she wasn't at the Doggie Diner, they took their paperwork to the library, worked until closing, and then went for coffee and late-night discussions with other protesters. At first, Liberty yielded to Gypsy's lead when asked about their views on the movement. She soon found her voice to be as strong as his.

The Berkeley Barb wrote an article on the April 15th, efforts. It explained the importance of Martin Luther King and James Bevel's involvement. The article included a photo of Liberty and Gypsy, side by side, flashing the peace sign in front of their recognizable van. The caption said, *Activists Liberty Carlson and Gypsy Forester are spreading the seeds of unrest for Mobe in the Bay area.*

In the picture, appeared the face of a woman whose life finally made sense—a woman at the beginning of her future.

# 36

A sore throat and head cold festered, then worsened as Liberty moved through the damp San Francisco weather on sheer willpower.

Ten days before the protest, a virus attacked her lungs. Midday, Gypsy slid open the door to the van to find her on the bed. She raised her head to study him and flopped back on the pillow. He touched her forehead.

Unnerved, he wrapped her in the granny-square afghan and drove to the Free Clinic on Clayton Street. Gypsy steadied her as they waited outside in line on the damp sidewalk for twenty minutes. When let in, he carried her upstairs to the crowded reception area.

They sat on floor pillows, waiting their turn beside shivering hippies and stoned dropouts. Liberty slept. Gypsy studied the discolored patterns on the stucco walls.

A clinic volunteer in a tie-dye shirt called Liberty's name. He led them to a small room with little more than a wooden examination table and three folding chairs.

Squinting through round rimless glasses, he said, "We mostly treat substance abuse and gonorrhea here."

"Are you a doctor?" Gypsy asked.

"Sorry, I'm a pharmacy student. I can't help you."

"What are you saying?" Liberty asked.

"The doctor's out. He'll be back in an hour, maybe two. You can wait here."

Liberty climbed onto the table, heaving out coughs followed by deep burning stabs in her chest. Gypsy paced the ten-foot room, the muscles in his jaw pulsing.

Wearing his lab coat over a Hawaiian shirt and camouflage pants, the doctor entered. After listening to her chest, he said, "You have a heavy case of lower lobe pneumonia. It's nothing to mess with. You need an x-ray and treatment right away. In a hospital."

Gypsy said, "We can't afford to go to a hospital."

The doctor gave him an understanding smile.

"Man, can't you do something?" Gypsy handed him a Mobe flyer. "She's on the team to put this together next Saturday."

"I'm involved with it, too. I'll be there for medical support."

"Then you know how important this is. Please help us."

The doctor studied Gypsy's face. "It's not ideal, but I can give her a limited supply of Rep samples."

"You'll help us?"

"Like I said, this is nothing to mess around with." He left and returned with three blister packs of ten Ampicillin capsules. "Four times a day. These will last her seven days."

Gypsy leaped from his chair. "Thank you."

"She's young and in good shape, but pneumonia's tricky. If she doesn't show signs of improvement in four days, you'll have to get her to a hospital whether you can afford it or not."

"I will. Thank you." Gypsy shook his hand.


The pace of the mobilization efforts had turned frantic. Gypsy knew he couldn't watch over her. Andrea and Sunshine came to the rescue. Liberty's closet room was still vacant. It offered a quiet place where he knew she'd be safe.

While she shivered on the bed, her clouded mind summoned the faint sounds of shoes on the stairs and her friends visiting with food. Memories of Gypsy checking on her floated past, but her burning chest, heavy eyes, and headaches continued.

Unpleasant dreams flooded her sleep, like North Forks engulfed in fire and alien creatures attaching themselves to Gypsy's van. In the most disturbing episode, a doorbell buzzed, commanding her to answer. She stumbled down a narrow hallway to the front door, to stop the noise. A blast of cold air pushed the door open. Her mother, dressed in a black felt cape and a veiled pillbox hat, grinned at her.

"You don't belong here," Liberty said.

Silhouetted against a gloomy evening, the woman laughed and brought a mother-of-pearl cigarette holder between two gloved fingers to her mouth. The smoldering ash dropped to the floor. "Who do you think you are, calling yourself Liberty?"

"It's a metaphor for freedom, you idiot. Freedom from you."

Her mother stood motionless, transformed into a marble statue. As Liberty reached to touch it, the stone groaned, crumbled into a heap of dust, and blew away.


The antibiotics eased her breathing by the fourth day, and her mind cleared. Although unsteady, she went into the kitchen.

"Liberty." Sunshine's mouth dropped open. "What are you doing?" She got up from the table. "You need to go back to bed."

"Do you know what day it is?"

"Sunday, the ninth."

"Shit. Only six days left." She turned and shuffled back to bed, cursing every hour that threatened to keep her from helping with the preparations.

The next day, still tired and weak, she called out, "Does anyone know what day it is?"

No one answered.

"I've got to get back to work." She laid back, reflecting on what the doctor had said. *She's young and in good shape.*

On the tip of sleep, she recited, *Everything I am going through is making me stronger. I am an unstoppable force of nature.*

Nothing would keep her from joining Gypsy on Thursday. Although she barely participated during their meetings with the Student Mobilization Committee and the local SDS chapters, being out of the apartment gave her strength and helped clear her head.

Toward the end of the day, they met Kate at Sparky's. She laid a thick notebook on the table to share its contents. They reviewed the revised roster of speakers and decided which position they would hold in the lineup.

They briefly discussed the bands committed and on board and all that needed to be taken care of before Saturday. As they parted, Kate said, "You look a little shaky, but I'm glad you're back."

In the evening, when Liberty took out her diary, she saw that Gypsy had filled in the days she missed.

# 37

# Harper

## 2020

On May 25, the Covid death count had reached 97,724. The number of deaths caused by police brutality went up—by one.

Not wanting to look, but feeling I had to, I watched a Minneapolis police officer smash his knee on the neck of a black man pinned to the pavement next to a cop car.

With his hands tucked in the pockets of his uniform pants, like he was checking for spare change, the cop's expression showed no compassion. He stared self-righteously at the bystanders filming the torture on their cell phones while three other officers stood by and watched George Floyd take his last breath.

My heart raced with the same feeling of helplessness I had when I saw Ahmaud Arbery dead on the road, and Philando Castile slumped in his car. Angry at myself, I could no longer hide in my house and brood about these things. The smugness and brutality lit my torch.

I texted Mateo.

He replied, *ILU making plans. back 2 u l8r.*

In the evening, he sent a group text with an Instagram link announcing a protest in downtown Atlanta at Centennial Olympic Park at 3 pm the next day. He added, *Meet@Ted Turner & Walton 1pm. We'll walk to park from there.*

He phoned a minute later.

"Fire, are you in?"

"Can I drive to your house and go with you?"

"Of course, yes. Are you sure?"

"Yes. I'm ready."

"My mom, Grams, Gramps, you, and me'll carpool together."

"I haven't met them yet."

"They'll love you, like I do."

"I hope so. Do they know this will be my first march?"

"They're thrilled you're a newbie. Someone to mentor." He laughed. "The most important thing is to wear comfortable shoes. And bring your face mask."

"Oh, I will. You know I will."

Uncle Kevin held me in a tender hug when I told him my plans.

"I figured as much when I saw the news. And I know you have to do this." He let go. "Just know if I had a vote, it would be for you to stay here, safe at home."

"I'm a little scared, but I can't not go. I can't just watch other people doing the right thing."

"I'm glad you'll be with Mateo. Just be careful."

"I'll be more than careful."

"Take Deja's number with you."

"Already put it in my phone."

I left at nine in the morning for the three-hour drive to Nashdale. The excitement of what the day might bring fought with my nervousness. I wrapped my hands so tight around the steering wheel they went numb.

The sun broke through the clouds as I passed the Perry exit, and I wondered if the grandparents I'd never known would have approved of my eagerness to join the protest. Further down the road, as I passed the billboard for The Southern Belly, I sensed Mama was with me. And Atticus, too. My nerves flared up again when I saw the "Nashdale, 25 Miles" sign.

When I turned onto Mateo's street lined with crape myrtle trees, four boys played in the front yard of one of the aged brick houses.

I had fantasized about his mother being like Erin Brockovich, a modern-day "David" going head to head with the big boys, all while raising her son. As I got closer to their address, my stomach tightened. I worried she wouldn't like me.

Like a bright star lighting the way, Mateo waved to me from the driveway. He opened the car door and slid his hand into mine.

"Come in the house," he said. "You can wear a mask if you want."

"Not now. I have to get over this hang-up."

When we stepped into the living room, his mother walked out of the kitchen toward me. Tall and blonde, she wore no makeup yet looked like she had stepped out of a television commercial. I hadn't seen a real mother so pretty. Her turquoise t-shirt said, *I can't breathe.*

"Mom, this is Harper."

"I'm so happy to meet you." Her hug felt warm. "I'm Rain."

"Rain?" I said, thinking I hadn't heard her right.

She nodded. "Yes. It's a side effect of having parents who were hippies. On my birth certificate, it says Rainbow, but when I turned ten, I begged them to call me Rain." She smiled warmly. "I'm glad you came."

"Thank you."

I looked at Mateo's brown-skinned face and flat nose. It took a lot of work to connect any features the two of them shared.

"I'll be right back," Rain said, leaving the room.

Being in the living room next to Mateo calmed me. A cluster of mismatched throw pillows covered the couch, and a beaded macramé decoration hung on the wall. Crossword puzzles, playing cards, and board games filled an open chest under a corner table.

"This is nice," I said to him.

Rain returned with a t-shirt over her arm. "Mateo said this is your first protest, so I got you an initiation gift." She handed me a Black Lives Matter shirt that matched Mateo's. She still wore her wedding ring.

"Do you want to make a sign?" she asked.

They had already made theirs and set them next to the front door. Mateo's said, NO JUSTICE, NO PEACE. Rain gave a lot more thought and time to hers. She had listed the names of people killed, each name written in a different color. George Floyd, in green. Breanna Taylor, in yellow. Michael Brown, in Brown. Philando Castile, purple. Sandra Bland, pink. Tamir Rice, blue.

There were eleven names in all. I didn't know some of them, but imagined she would have kept going if there had been more room.

"Cardboard and markers are in the den," she said.

Using a black marker, I kept it simple. BLACK LIVES MATTER, with an exclamation mark, and set it by the front door next to theirs.

"You must be starving after the drive here," Rain said. "I have a pot of soup on the stove. We can leave after we eat."

A blue farm table chipped with years of use dominated the kitchen. I pictured Mateo as a kid doing his homework there. Rain placed a cutting board on the table, with slices of bread from a crusty loaf and a softened cube of butter. Then, three bowls of vegetable soup with bits of Italian parsley on top.

"I'm nervous," I said, buttering my bread.

"Don't worry," Mateo said.

"The weatherman said it'll reach eighty-two today," Rain said. "Be sure to drink water. I have extra in my backpack, and snacks."

"I didn't think about that."

"It's fine, I have plenty."

"You brought a mask?"

"Two," I said, self-consciously. Actually, there were three.

Mateo said, as casually as if it was a typical day, "After we meet our group, we'll hear some speeches, march to the Capitol, and then go back to the park before heading home."

Rain took another slice of bread. "Harper, sometimes a protest can go sideways quickly, so pay attention." She smiled. "Even with your very visible red hair, getting lost in the crowd is easy. Rule number one is, always stay together."

She put her hand on my arm. "We're the support team for the Minneapolis protesters. Showing solidarity is our duty."

I nodded. The word duty stuck in my ears. I worried I wouldn't be up to the task.

In Liberty's diary, she wrote about Jackie, the woman she admired so much. The crazy thought hit me. Rain was my Jackie.

She carried our bowls and spoons to the sink and turned off the flame under the pot. "My parents have an annoying habit of quoting Gandhi," she said. "Their favorite is, 'The future depends on what we do in the present.'"

"They do a lot of quoting," Mateo said. "I like the one from Steinbeck."

I wanted to say my mother quoted Atticus Finch a lot, but instead asked when Mateo's grandparents would be there?"

"Grams came down with a bug, and Gramps is staying home to take care of her."

"Hope it's not Covid," I said.

Mateo shook his head at me. "You're my Little Miss Covid Crazy."

"I know. I worry too much."

# 38

Once in Atlanta, the still air seemed thick with importance like it was braced for anything. I watched collections of people crowd together and even through my mask, I smelled the stench of gasoline vapors and bus diesel.

Five men and three women greeted us at the corner of Turner and Walton, anxious and ready to soldier on. They had all been to previous BLM marches together. Mateo shook their hands and introduced me. I did the same, invigorated by their commitment.

We walked toward the park like Olympians marching to the stadium. Police stood around the perimeter. Once inside, we wound past the Magnolia Tribute Garden to the pavilion near the Ferris wheel. In the park, the city smells turned more gentle. Thousands had gathered, milling around in their masks and holding signs. I hadn't expected to see so many white people.

A sound crew hooked up microphones and loudspeakers on a temporary stage. A little before 3 pm, one of the organizers took to the microphone to welcome everyone. After thanking what seemed to be all the bigwigs in Atlanta, he called for a moment of silence.

A hush covered the space. We raised our fists in the air. I looked up at the sky as clouds lazily crossed above us. Then I looked at Mateo. With the sun highlighting the purple streaks, his hair resembled a tribal headdress. His dark eyes were serious.

One by one, local politicians filled the stage. A congresswoman from the Atlanta area said, "Never forget, protesting is as important as voting." She spoke louder. "And never forget to vote, vote, vote." The crowd shouted their approval and echoed back, *vote, vote, vote.*

I asked Mateo, "How many people are going to talk?"

"A lot."

One man spoke about proposed hate crimes legislation, another about police reform. The last man on stage thanked us for our solidarity in battling violence against black Americans, and he told us to stay six feet apart to prevent the spread of COVID-19.

No one took note of his advice as everyone left the park chanting, "*We gon' be alright... We gon' be alright.*"

As we walked out of the park, I asked Mateo what *We gon' be alright* meant.

"Do you know Kendrick Lamar's song, *Alright?*"

"Sure, I know it."

"It's the movement's anthem."

"I didn't know that."

"The song's for us, the people here. The people on the streets doing the work. *We gon' be alright,* says we have faith things will be okay. Kinda like *We Shall Overcome* in the '60s."

Like Mateo had said, we headed down Marietta toward the Capitol. Protest signs stretched to the horizon. Many were portraits of Floyd, honoring him with more than words. A local television station helicopter hovered. Cops flanked the side streets.

I held my sign high and thought of how Liberty and Gypsy marched together through the streets of San Francisco. And like them, Mateo and I were shoulder-to-shoulder for the good. My imagined connection with Liberty was on overdrive. My chest swelled with pride.

When we got to the bronze statue of Henry Grady at Marietta and Forsyth, a woman with a bullhorn chanted, "No Justice, No Peace." We in the crowd answered, "No Racist Police." My feet hit the pavement with the rhythm of the back-and-forth exchange that went on for blocks. "No Justice, No Peace."

"No Racist Police."

"There she is," I said, pointing. Atop the dome of the Capital stood the statue of Miss Freedom holding her torch and sword.

"More speeches?" I asked Mateo.

"I don't see any equipment set up. We'll just chill for a while."

People of every shade, age, and background had collected peacefully. My feelings overwhelmed me, and I imagined Mama and Liberty standing by my side.

On our way back to the park, tension filled the air. The crowd moved differently. Some of the people yelled, "fuck you assholes," and "cops are pigs," and worse. My excitement vanished, replaced by fear.

Peaceful protesters threw their signs on the ground and held up their cell phones. Rain put her hand on my shoulder and told me to drop my sign.

As we passed the Henry Grady statue again, close to fifty people were on the lower platform, their fists high, their voices angry

*KILL PIGS!* was sprayed in red paint across the base, and the letters *KKK* were at the top of the pedestal. On the street near the statue, a man in a black bandana mask and skull cap knocked down several steel crowd barriers.

Wearing yellow and black shirts, the bicycle cops gathered across the width of Marietta Street, blocking the crowd from passing.

Someone yelled, "Pepper spray."

"Take my hand," Rain shouted. She led me off the street to the sidewalk, where we could move more quickly. We rushed past the bike cops and made it beyond the immediate commotion. An explosion erupted behind us. I turned to look back. A police car had burst into flames. I smelled the stench of the black smoke. Rain's hand gripped mine tighter.

"Fast," she said, and we hauled ass. Mateo was steps behind us. When I saw the tension on their faces, I panicked. My eyes blurred, and the toe of my shoe caught on a crack in the sidewalk. I went down on my knees. My palms slid across the concrete and my head smacked the ground.

Mateo lifted me onto my feet and held on as I hobbled to the park and settled on a bench. Adrenaline delayed the pain in my hands and knees, but my lungs burned.

I called Uncle Kevin as soon as I could, hoping he hadn't seen any news about the protest.

"You know what to do. Leave a message."

"I'm okay. I'm safe. Don't worry," I said, then added, "In case you're watching the news, I'm nowhere near the trouble. I'll call you when we get back to Mateo's house."

We barely spoke during the drive to Nashdale, each of us in our own thoughts. I sat in the backseat behind Rain, studying her soft, blond hair. Next to her, Mateo's fingers barely left his phone.

With the smell of smoldering rubber still in my memory, I tried to close my mind to the defeat I felt. It seemed Mateo and his mother were doing the same.

When halfway to Nashdale, Uncle Kevin called. The raw worry in his voice reached my heart. I thought about all the family he had lost and how he had stood up and made the sacrifices—done the right thing. I did my best to sound upbeat and assured him we had steered clear of the danger and were on our way home.

In the kitchen, Mateo picked tiny bits of gravel out of my bloody knees using tweezers and a magnifying glass. Rain dabbed them with rubbing alcohol. While they worked on my knees, I smeared ointment on my scraped hands. The bump on my head was the size of a quarter and tender to the touch.

We swallowed defeat and held a vigil from the couch, watching the news. The looters had breached the CNN building and broken every window. A line of police stood deeper inside as protection.

"Why are they doing this?" I said over and over, each time feeling the same anger.

"Sometimes outsider groups—thugs—see a protest as an opportunity to loot and destroy in all the confusion," Rain said. "It's always a setback. My mom says, 'We were meant to survive and tell our stories,' and I've taken that to mean, be smart, be strong, and don't let the assholes overtake the cause." She patted my thigh. "Take what happened today with you and learn."

"They hijacked our peaceful protest. How am I going to let this go?"

"The struggle is the victory."

At 10 pm, the mayor of Atlanta asked the crowd to disperse, saying, "What I see happening on the streets of Atlanta is not Atlanta. This is not a protest. This is not in the spirit of Martin Luther King, Jr." She paused. "This is chaos."

# 39

# Liberty

# 1967

They woke long before daylight.

"How are you feeling?" Gypsy asked.

"Still weak, but I can breathe better. Today is a mind-over-matter day."

"April 15th," Gypsy said, his smile brimming. "I didn't sleep last night."

Liberty drove Sweet Pea down the dark, fog covered San Francisco streets. She dropped Gypsy off at Second and Market, the starting point of the march to the stadium. A handful of men from The American Federation of Teachers' local 1570 greeted him. They would be in the lead, carrying a banner the width of the street.

His morning task was to connect with the different locals and groups to help secure their places in the line, and make sure the march started on time.

As Liberty drove off, the sky turned pink, and the sun streamed through the clouds. She went to Bernie's apartment to carpool with him and Kate to Kezar in Bernie's VW Bug.

Wound up, Bernie tapped his fist against the steering wheel. He chain-smoked and swore at every red light. Kate rode shotgun, working on revisions to her opening speech. Liberty sat in the back, feeling nauseous, with her hands over her face to escape the cigarette smoke.

"Today has to be so enormous," Bernie said. "And so significant that every motherfucking madman in D.C. will be shitting his pants."

"It's going to be," Kate said sarcastically, and added, "Let the shitting begin."

The three of them walked into the stadium through the chilly tunnel at the east end of the field, seven hours before the 2:45 pm starting time. Once inside, Liberty stopped to take in the enormity of the place, and the day. Her admiration for these people and their total commitment to the movement overwhelmed her. Kate and Bernie left to meet with Ed Keating, Jerry, and several other organizers huddled on the infield.

A group of priests with umbrellas entered the stadium as if they were on a morning stroll. Soon, more people and families with kids in strollers arrived. They, too, were seven hours early.

Her assignment was to coordinate with the crew and sound technicians to set up the stage. They had brought plywood and poles and their sound equipment to the middle of the field. In a light rain, she watched them skillfully construct the platform without a glitch. Attached to all four corners of the stage were poles topped with stadium speakers, facing out to broadcast in all four directions.

Her mind wandered. *What if the speakers malfunction and there is no sound? What if the stage collapses under the weight of so many people?* She caught herself being negative and blamed it on the lingering effects of pneumonia. *Negative thoughts do not serve me anymore.*

After the side rails went up and stairs were attached, she climbed them, cursing her burning chest and fighting back a coughing jag. She walked to center stage and surveyed the field, thinking of all the people who would be there as comrades-in-arms, signing up and reporting for duty on the Spring Mobilization battlefield.

They were not a flock of sheep but a tribe determined to have their voices heard. They carried the most necessary element of the day—purpose.

Around 11 am, the marchers with Gypsy entered the stadium, galvanized and ready to take on the main event. Eager photographers rushed to get in front of them to capture the scene.

Counter-demonstrators circled the track with signs saying *Support Our Men in Vietnam*, and

*Communism is Red Fascism.* A roar of boos rose from the arena, followed by a full-on brawl. Liberty couldn't find Gypsy in the crowd. It didn't take long before the Longshoremen security volunteers rounded up everyone involved in the brawl and ushered them off the grounds.

All 62,000 of the stadium seats were filled. Thousands of stragglers stood on the track and infield, and more than 10,000 latecomers gathered outside. Before then, the Human-Be-In had been the largest crowd Liberty had ever seen.

With the heaviness in her chest growing, she struggled to slide the lectern to the front of the stage. Wobbling, she opened one of the fifteen folding chairs stacked on the platform to sit in and catch her breath, worried she might faint.

Gypsy saw her struggle and went up to joined her. He set up the remaining chairs, and helped her down to the grass area by one of the speakers.

"You're my White Rabbit," she said.

He gave her a quizzical look.

"I followed you into this wonderland."

Kate proudly accompanied the VIPs past her and Gypsy and up to their designated chairs. They remained standing, chests high, eyes scanning the crowd. After ten minutes of cheering, the union leaders, civil rights superstars, politicians, and scholars took their seats. Keating and Kate sat among them.

Judy Collins had been one of the first singers to oppose the war publicly. Kate's chair was between her and Coretta Scott King.

At 3:00 pm, she took her papers to the podium. Liberty watched, overwhelmed with pride, remembering Jackie's comment about activists being the shining lights of our democracy.

Kate introduced herself and thanked the crowd for their support. She paused. "But there's one section of American youth who aren't with us in the stadium today. They aren't in the New York rally either. Those are the ones who have been drafted to fight this dirty war in Vietnam. But because they aren't with us today, we cannot assume—and indeed we must not assume—they are against us."

The crowd erupted with earsplitting approval. Nothing in her life had prepared Liberty for such an enormous moment.

Kate continued, "We are here to demonstrate our belief that the soldiers have the right to protest the war in Vietnam. We're extending our hands to them and taking a lesson from the students who have been making attempts to build links with them. We are joining with the soldiers in their demand that they be brought home now."

Floating in waves of lightheadedness, Liberty celebrated Kate's speech along with nearly one-hundred-thousand others.

"At this time," Kate said. "It's my honor to introduce you to our keynote speaker, Master

Sergeant Donald Duncan, our nation's first Vietnam Vet to oppose the war publicly." Cheers traversed the stadium. "His article in *Ramparts* is a must-read. If you haven't read it yet, you will after you hear what he has to say today."

After Duncan denounced the government's escalation in Vietnam, Julian Bond revealed that one out of every ten young men in America is a Negro, but two out of every five men killed in Vietnam is a Negro.

David Harris announced the formation of a new group of draft protesters called *The Resistance*. He proposed everyone mail their draft cards back to the government in protest of an unjust and immoral war.

With his arm around Liberty to steady her, Gypsy said, "This guy's the real deal. The face of the resistance."

Eldridge Cleaver, Morris Evenson, and Robert Vaughn each took their turn solidifying the message all the people gathered knew—the Vietnam War was wrong.

When Coretta Scott King rose to speak, a hush blanketed the stadium, followed by deafening admiration. A large white corsage covered the lapel of her dark coat. She showed undeniable strength and forcefulness when speaking of non-violence and commitment to global peacemaking.

With no hysteria or fear, every speech gave the attendees ideas and proclamations to walk away with. In response, their applause spread over the walls and spilled across the Bay Area.

After the speeches and music had ended, Liberty and Gypsy joined the committee members, and a smattering of volunteers on the stage. Under heavy clouds ready to shed more rain, they watched the gatherers exit the stadium with optimism.

Drained and feeling worse, Liberty wasn't sure whether she was hallucinating or not when she spotted someone who looked like Rachael Nolan walking toward her. She leaned on Gypsy and fainted.

# 40

# Harper

# 2020

Mateo had wanted my first march to be memorable, but not in the way it turned out. As I left the following morning, he handed me his copy of Patrisse Cullors *When They Call You a Terrorist, A Black Lives Matter Memoir*.

"It's an eye-opener," he said. "When you read it you'll understand more and see the greatness of her energy."

On the way home, the ache of my scraped knees and hands helped feed my disappointment. I knew we were doing good. We were there to stand up against injustice. Most of the assholes went to jail, but I still had trouble thinking positively about it.

Uncle Kevin stood on the front porch like a sentry keeping vigil. "The wounded warrior returns," he said as I got out of the car and limped up the stairs. Filled with emotion, I wrapped my arms around him.

"I gotta admit, you had me worried, Harper."

"I'm sorry. Seeing that stuff on television, I would have been worried too. Just know, Mateo and his mom took perfect care of me."

"It's a good thing, or I'd have to kick his ass."

"They're pros. They've been protesting for years. Even his grandparents."

"I talked with Deja this morning."

"Washington?"

He nodded with a slight smile.

"First name basis now? You sweet on her?"

"Come inside," he said. "I made lunch."

On the table, egg salad sandwiches, pickles, and BBQ chips were on paper plates and covered with plastic wrap. We sat down, and once I started talking, it all spilled out with hardly a pause, from arriving at Mateo's house straight through to the car exploding. He let me ramble.

"You know what I liked the best about the whole experience?"

"Nope," he said, finishing the chips.

"I wasn't there for myself." I took a minute to choose my words. "Because I'd never be beaten and jailed, or kicked in the face, or killed for a traffic stop, or a counterfeit twenty dollar bill."

Uncle Kevin raised his eyebrows and nodded.

"I was there to help others get justice and to be

respected the way I would be. And, you know what else is cool?"

"Nope," he said and tilted his head.

"You don't need a special skill or a degree to commit to bringing about justice and humanity for all." My shoulders rose, and my hands opened. "Yesterday was a real turning point for me." Finally, I began to eat.

"I'm proud of you, and I know Ellie would be bursting at the seams."

Hearing her name caused my chest to pinch, and the sting in my eyes forced me to close them and let the tears fall. "I think I'll go to my place," I said, realizing the toll the past twenty-four hours had taken.

After two hours of sleep, I woke to a constant replay of the protest in my head. I picked up the phone to call Megan but realized it wasn't her I wanted to share my feelings with. It was Liberty.

Plucking the diary from the nightstand, I spoke to it in hushed tones. "I know you know exactly how I feel today. I forgot to tell Uncle Kevin how being there boosted my pride and self-confidence. It's dumb saying these things to your diary, but I wish we could have been there together." I opened it and read through it again.

The next morning, I went to the garden. Seeing each sprout of lettuce felt like a little win. Each yellow blossom that morphed into a tomato or zucchini brought success. Each bean pod was a masterpiece.

I talked to Charlotte as I weeded. "It's war," I said. "We have to protect our little treasures against these bullies that want to take over."

Chirping sparrows watched over me from Charlotte's branches as I checked under healthy leaves for unwanted aphids and cucumber beetles, and tossed them into a jar of soapy water. And, like always, I took comfort in the feel of the dirt and the fresh air.

Mateo's ringtone chimed on my phone.

"Hey," I answered.

"We had to take Grams to the hospital," he said in a panic. "She couldn't breathe. They put her in the ICU. She has Covid."

"Oh my God. Are you there?"

"They won't let us stay. I'm in the parking lot, bringing the car to the front to pick up my mom and Gramps. We have to quarantine for ten days."

I hadn't heard him sound scared before.

Knowing that four days earlier, the death toll had reached the milestone of 100,000, I began to pace. I'd been hearing more and more stories of people dying alone in the ICU, too sick to know what was happening to them. And when the end came, they had nothing more than a FaceTime call with family to share their last moments.

"Stay safe," I said when I should have told him I

love him. Stay safe sounded like an order from my Covid-crazy mind.

"You said it when she got sick. You were right, Harper."

We FaceTimed every evening. I mostly listened. Being quarantined while feeling perfectly fine was hard for him. During each call, he began with the latest update on his grandmother's condition. The nursing staff gave them hope to hang on to, even though she wasn't improving. The worry had definitely stressed him out.

To calm his mind, he broke down the meaning and themes behind the stories in his favorite books.

"You know Hemingway's *The Old Man and the Sea*?"

"Uh-huh," I said. I knew who Hemingway was but had never read any of his books.

"You know how Santiago keeps having dreams of lions in Africa?"

Confused, I said, "Lions? Wait, what?" *I thought it took place in the ocean.*

"I think the dreams trigger memories of when he was young and strong. The dreams kind of give him the mental strength to triumph against all the shit thrown at him."

Even more confused, I let him talk it out, moving from one idea to the next.

"And you remember how he suffered with his messed-up hands by bringing the Marlin home? And how he looked up to Joe DiMaggio for inspiration?"

"Joe DiMaggio, seriously?"

I finally told him I hadn't read the book.

"You should. My dad loved that book. It's sort of a fable, and it's short. You can get through it in a day or two."

"Okay. I'll check it out."

"So, Santiago's an old fisherman with an old boat who finds himself up against a gigantic Marlin. He fishes with his bare hands, which makes it this epic win until the Marlin drags him so far out to sea that it takes three days to get back to shore.

"Really?" I said, not convinced I'd like it.

"It's about much more than that. It's about struggle, and what it means to be human. And never giving up even when things totally suck. The old man never gives up hope."

The next evening, he analyzed Andy Dufrense's plight in *Rita Hayworth and Shawshank Redemption*. I was thankful I'd seen the movie with Tim Robbins and Morgan Freeman.

"Like Santiago's tiny boat," Mateo said, "Andy's dinky little rock hammer symbolized that no matter how crappy things are, it's your determination that matters more than anything. Triumph has more to do with perseverance than the equipment you use."

I wanted to say my favorite part of the movie was when they discovered the hole he'd dug, but didn't want to interrupt him.

Point by point, he moved from Warden Norton, to Brooks and his bird, then on to Red. I finally got comfortable with these conversations being the way he coped, and was happy to listen and agree.

# 41

The next morning after Mateo had talked through the loss of innocence and the other metaphors weaved through *Catcher in the Rye*, he called early.

"It's over. Grandma Libby died."

"Oh, no." I slumped and looked out the window toward Charlotte's swaying branches. At first, I thought I'd imagined what he said. Not that she had passed, but her name. Had I heard him right? Was it a coincidence or could it be possible?

"I'm so sorry," I said, lost in my distraction.

Mateo's voice cracked several times. "When they called, it felt like a punch in the stomach. Then, there was nothing. I didn't get to say goodbye. Nobody did except the nurse. I have to go. My mom needs me. I just wanted to let you know."

"What can I do?"

"Nothing right now. I need a little time alone."

More stunned about his grandma's name than upset with his anguish, I rushed to the nightstand, grabbed the diary, and stared at it. I felt dizzy.

*Did he say, Grandma Libby?*

After Mama died, I went through some off-the-deep-end irrational thinking, but this was more bonkers.

My skin turned clammy, and a layer of crazy washed over me—the kind of crazy in fantastical dreams, yet possible.

I might have been in more shock than Mateo. *Was his grandpa Gypsy?*

Because the Covid restrictions made it impossible to gather mourners in a hall for a memorial service, they struggled to figure out how to celebrate her the way she deserved.

"Nobody's having funerals," I said.

"I know." He sounded miserable. "Even if we planned something, no one could come."

With only one thing on my mind, I had to ask. "Mateo, did you say your grandma's name is Libby?"

"Yeah, that's her name. Listen, I've got another call coming in. Can I get back to you?"

It was too bizarre without proof and too unlikely, even though my heart wanted it to be true.

Remembering I'd seen Gypsy's last name somewhere in the diary, I flipped through it and found:

October 14, 1967—Saturday.

*Packing up is bittersweet. I told Gypsy I think the name Libby feels more genuine to me, and I want to leave Liberty behind. He agrees.*

*He doesn't feel Gypsy fits him anymore, either. We're leaving S. F. as Libby Carlson, and John Forester. Next stop, Virginia, to march on the Pentagon.*

The following day, Mateo sounded less stressed. "We're going to set up a livestream tribute. My buddy David will walk me through the technical stuff."

He said they scheduled it for Sunday, June 14th, two weeks after she passed, and I still wasn't absolutely, positively sure.

Mateo posted an invitation on Facebook and Twitter to join the livestream Celebration of Life for Elizabeth "Libby" Forester, January 14, 1949 - June 1, 2020.

Even though I had wanted it to be so, my chest tightened, and the sadness of a personal loss slammed into me like a bulldozer.

I ran scenarios through my head about how to tell Mateo what I finally knew for sure. They all began with, "You're not going to believe this, but..."

A sore throat, runny nose, and chest cough blew up my plans to be there with him.

Because Uncle Kevin knew it meant a lot to me,

he set up his laptop on the coffee table in front of the couch and logged on. We sat beside each other. I had the diary on my lap.

"What's that?" Uncle Kevin asked.

"I'll tell you when the service is over."

"What is it?"

"Shh, it's starting." I pressed the diary to my chest while crying and laughing at the same time.

"You're freaking me out. What's going on?"

"Shush. It's too weird. I'll tell you when this is over."

Rain stood behind the podium wearing a black t-shirt that said RESIST and PERSIST.

"I want to thank every one of you who is out there joining us from your phones, computer screens, and Smart TVs, for sharing this time with us."

She paused, took a deep breath, and stood tall. "As you all know, on June first, my mother was strangled by the talons of the heinous monster, COVID-19. She was in the ICU unit of Southern Regional Medical Center, technically alone, but love surrounded her.

"All of you, her friends and students, know she was the force who inspired me toward a life of activism. I'm dressed in this shirt—her shirt—in her honor."

She cleared her throat. "Since she was eighteen, my mother has fought for social justice. She volunteered to help the homeless, carried rainbow flags at PrideFests, hammered nails to build houses, raised money, and wrote letters to Congress. Her steadfastness was legendary." Rain looked toward the camera. "Mom, I promise to keep your legacy alive."

I remembered having soup in Rain's kitchen and how being near her calmed me.

Mateo's grandfather moved slowly toward her. My heart leaped. The necklace, strung with silver arrowheads and turquoise beads, hung over the lapels of his black suit. His hair looked like a white halo. He hugged his daughter before she stepped aside.

A heavy sigh launched his tribute.

"Thank you, everyone, for coming. I'm not prepared for this moment, as I never imagined my girl wouldn't always be by my side."

He pulled a folded piece of paper from his suit pocket, spread it out on the flat surface in front of him, and rubbed his hands over the creases.

"Courage and strength," he said. "Lib had both. If all were right with the world, there would be no need for either. Wouldn't that be nice."

He paused. "The evening Lib thought she was coming down with a cold, we decided not to go to the George Floyd protest the next day. Instead of marching, she wrote this at the breakfast table." He fiddled with his glasses.

"Today, when the opposition attempts to block the young justice fighters, it is important that they know about the previous generations who also prevailed over ignorance and fear.

"Just as my generation took courage from those in whose footsteps we followed, the Standing Rock: Water is Life, and Black Lives Matter leaders show us the strength we can get from those whose battles paved the way for us over generations and centuries. We are the history and the future, both of which are grounded in a vision that feeds us, and makes our lives rich."

He took off his glasses, blotted his eyes with a tissue, and managed a faint smile. "This message is quintessential Lib."

His eyebrows knitted together. "We have several scrapbooks filled with clippings of hundreds of Letters to the Editor she wrote. Only a handful of people know they were hers because she wrote under the pseudonym May Bloom, in order to speak with candor on some of her more controversial beliefs while shielding her family and the Forester name from the extremists."

*May Bloom, I thought. That's why Googling her was a bust.*

He leaned forward and smiled. "To be sure, Lib wasn't always a saint. Case in point, the Georgia Bulldogs is the team she chose to worship."

He said *The Giant Spider Invasion* was her favorite movie, and that once during a trip to Mexico, after drinking a bottle of Monte Alban Mezcal, she took her clothes off and climbed into the town square fountain." His eyes welled.

He shared how they met. "In Golden Gate Park, on Lib's eighteenth birthday, at the beginning of." He used air quotes. "The Summer of Love." He smiled into the camera. "Love—and protest. It was a sweet, magical time that changed the world."

I already knew all this. They met at the Human Be-In. I had read about it many times.

It took a minute before he said, "So, how did we get from there to here? Good question."

He said the San Francisco scene had morphed into a bizarre cartoon crammed with more and more people who didn't have a purpose or give a damn about anything. It lost its luster, and they decided to leave for good to look for another place to settle. He said they took over a year trying out a few towns, but nothing felt right until they got to Georgia.

"Why Georgia?" His voice wobbled. "As Lib would say, 'It was the dogwoods.' About a half hour's drive into the state, on the right side of the road, we passed a field of them exploding with white blossoms." He closed his eyes at the thought. "A breathtaking sight. A vision as white and pure as the soft clouds above. We stopped the van and got out to take in the light honeysuckle fragrance. Lib said, 'This is it. I can't imagine living anywhere else.'"

He said they settled in Hickory Springs for a few months until Mayor Allen's team hired him as an Assistant City Manager.

"Atlanta suited us well, and Lib got her teaching degree. That was 47 years ago. I naively imagined there would be many more years together, but you know what they say, if you want to make God laugh, tell him your plans." He backed up and stepped out of the camera's view.

I closed my eyes, and like so many times in the past two weeks, I couldn't get over how close I felt to the woman I'd never met, and now never will.

"I know her," I said.

Uncle Kevin frowned. "Who?"

"Libby."

"Who?"

"Mateo's grandma."

"How?"

"I'll tell you later. Here comes Mateo." I pointed to the screen.

There he was. Seeing him took my breath. He wore a leather jacket over a plain white t-shirt. In that moment, I finally realized how seriously, deeply, and incredibly in love I was. He licked his lips, cleared his throat, and began.

"I'm Mateo, the lucky boy who didn't have to share his grandma with any other grandkids."

He licked his lips. "Grandma Libby cared more than most and loved more than most. She loved without condition and was always ready with a hug.

"I remember when I was six, she took me to a small protest against banned books at a school library. Instead of signs, we carried books. She held up a copy of *The Adventures of Huckleberry Finn,* and I had *Draw Me a Star.* I still have that book.

"Afterward, we walked to a park. When I told her I was afraid to climb the ladder to the slide, she said she knew how I felt. 'I used to be afraid of things, too,' she said, 'until I figured out the secret.' I asked, What secret?

"She squatted to get eye level with me and put her hands on my shoulders. 'One rung is easy,' she said. 'Concentrate on one rung at a time.'

"She waited at the bottom, arms stretched, telling me I could do it. I found the courage to get to the top and slide down. She is my inspiration, one rung at a time."

He shook his head. "Yes, she's gone, but what I inherited from her can't be damaged, destroyed, or lost."

Mateo smiled. "Today is the first time I heard about her Mezcal story. Tomorrow, I'll buy a bottle. Thank you all for coming."

I fantasized about being there with him, stepping up to the podium, and honoring her. My eulogy might have gone something like, "Without knowing, the things she wrote down in 1967 helped a stranger in need. It's been one year and one month to the day since I found her diary. It comforted me and helped me cope with losing my mama. Who could have imagined how the universe came up with such an unlikely coincidence?"

But I wasn't there. And it was clear the diary didn't belong to me anymore. I'd soon have to let it go.

Mateo, his mother, and grandfather were back in front of the camera, ending the ceremony. Rain said, "We encourage all of you to comment in the chat."

I might have gone into a trance or some other loony tunes condition. How else could I explain myself and the eighteen-year-old Libby, or Liberty, sitting in a coffee shop with one very long table? I had to squint to see her.

I asked, "Will you teach me how to make sure my life will have meaning?"

"One rung at a time," she said, then faded away.

It might have been five seconds or one minute before I heard my heart pounding. I was back on Uncle Kevin's couch, really shook up.

Confusion spread across his face. "So, you said you know Mateo's grandmother? How?"

"I'm not sure you'll believe it because I'm not sure I do. But, this is what happened." I told him everything, from Mama guiding me into the Second Chance, and Liberty teaching me the importance of having meaning in my life, to the phone call when Mateo said her name. I talked about all she had gone through in her childhood and in San Francisco, and I told him I'd promised both her and Mama it would be only our secret.

"I'd like to read it," he said. "Would that be alright?"

"Of course."

# 42

It had been a week since the memorial, and I still hadn't told Mateo. How could I? Very little made sense to me. I had long talks with Charlotte, which led nowhere.

The internet wasn't any help until a blog post titled *The Value of Family* triggered me to stop and read it.

The author wrote, "Family provides us with support, encouragement, love, and a place we can return to."

*Okay, genius, tell me something I don't know.* And there it was in the next sentence. "Our family roots often extend beyond what we can see."

I'd finally gotten the green light to go into the world where the things around me were both real and not real. I took the words *often extend beyond what we see* to mean spirits and ghosts are still family.

Whether they've been killed by a global pandemic, in a head-on accident, or an overdose, they care and look after us. They direct us to places that will help us overcome, and send messages from beyond, just like Mama did.

The drive to Nashdale was heavy with purpose. I kept my eyes on the freeway signs, one after another, so many directions to go. So many feelings to feel. So much anticipation.

Uncle Kevin gripped the steering wheel with intent. "I'm gonna ask one more time before we get too far," he said. "You ready for this?"

Just hearing the question made me uncertain.

He asked, "What do you think will happen when you show them?"

"No clue. Ten fingers crossed it will be good. I told Mateo we we're bringing them a surprise that had to do with his Grandma, and to invite his grandpa. Of course, he threw a thousand questions at me, but I kept strong."

Out of the blue Uncle Kevin said, "Do you know what today is?"

"Saturday."

"Summer solstice."

"I forgot what that is."

"When the sun's at its highest point. This is going to be a stellar day."

"I hope you're right, but what does the sun have to do with it?"

"It's a turning point each year. New chapters and all that."

"Are you getting weird on me?"

"That diary has given you everything you needed from it. Time to let go."

"I know. I'm ready." I patted my purse and felt its bulk inside.

Mateo greeted us out front—a fist bump for Uncle Kevin, a hug for me. He asked that we wear masks. Since his grandma died, they wore masks whenever they were with his grandpa.

Rain, beautiful as before, welcomed us into the living room. A large bouquet of dogwoods, sat on the coffee table, and calla lilies lined the mantel.

Mr. Forester came in from the kitchen. A white apron covered his sweatshirt and casual pants. Seeing him made me feel light-headed, and the knot in my stomach tightened. I knew what he looked like from the livestream, but meeting him in person was like having a fictional character from a beloved story come to life.

His eyes were bright and engaged. He ran his fingers through his winter-white hair, then opened his arms.

"So this is Mateo's beautiful redheaded girl. It's good to finally meet you."

"You, too, Mr. Forester. And this is my Uncle Kevin."

Knowing I needed to wait for the right time, I squeezed my eyes shut and held back the urge to pull the diary out of my bag, put it in his hands, and call him Gypsy.

"Have a seat," Rain said, motioning to the couch. "Dad made cookies. I'll be right back."

I cradled my purse between myself and Uncle Kevin. Mateo sat next to me. His grandpa chose one of the wingback chairs.

Mateo put his arm over my shoulder. "So, what's this big surprise you have for us?"

"I..." My mouth went dry just as Rain came back into the room carrying a tray of cookies.

"Mateo, can you move the dogwoods, please?" she asked. "I have chocolate chip and oatmeal raisin made this morning, by my favorite baker and father."

Uncle Kevin took an oatmeal raisin. To help prolong the inevitable, he talked about how nice the drive to Nashdale was, and then he mentioned how much he enjoyed the way they handled the Celebration of Life.

"Thanks," Mateo said. "It was tough, but it helped us get past the hard days and brought in some good memories."

I had drifted off to the place in my mind I'd been before, where I told them about the diary, and they told me it wasn't the same Libby.

Rain interrupted my head trip. "So, Harper, you don't ever need a reason to come visit, but Mateo said you have something for us that has to do with my mother."

"Well, yes, I do."

"The mystery has us intrigued."

After two days of rehearsing what I'd say, nothing came to mind. I reached into my purse, brought the diary out, and held it in front of me like it was a trophy.

Neither Mateo or Rain had any reaction. Mr. Forester narrowed his eyes. His brows held the weight of confusion as if a memory had tapped him on the shoulder and was close enough to live again. He pointed to it and rose from the chair.

"Mr. Forester," I said and stood up. "This is for you." I handed the diary across the coffee table and gave it to its rightful owner.

He traced his hand over the lettering and he carefully opened the worn cover. His fingers trembled slightly. "My God, where did you get this?"

"What is it?" Rain asked.

"It's your mother's diary from the time we met."

"What?" she said and looked at me.

"This is where we began," he said. "When we were young and full of dreams." He closed it gently and held it to his chest as if he could feel her, the same way I had in the loft of the thrift shop. He shut his eyes.

"I never heard about her diary before," Rain said.

"How do you have it?" Mateo said.

"I found it in a shop called Second Chance a little over a year ago."

"Before we even met?" Mateo said, puzzled.

In a jumble of emotions, I nodded my head. "I don't know how, but through some kind of weird, psycho fate, I opened the drawer of a nightstand, and there it was."

Feeling off balance, I sat back down on the couch.

"A nightstand?" Mr. Forester asked.

"Yes. With a logo on the back that said AFR."

"AFR Rental? Do they still exist?" He also sat down. Confusion crossed his face. "American Furniture Rental?" We rented three rooms of furniture from them when we lived in Hickory Springs, back in." he paused to remember. "1968."

"You rented furniture?" Mateo said, puzzled.

"We lived in the van for a year and didn't have much, so we signed a six-month contract for the furniture, hoping we could save up to buy our own. It turns out we left for Atlanta close to the same time the contract ended. AFR picked everything up and drove it off."

"I'm blown away," Rain said. "Blown away. How can this be?"

"Gramps, can I see it?"

Mateo opened it as carefully as if he were disengaging a bomb. His face stayed neutral as he turned the pages one by one, shaking his head and stopping to read some of it.

"It's her handwriting, alright."

He handed it to Rain.

"What a strange happiness I'm feeling right now. This is going to take some time to process," she said and set the diary on her lap without opening it.

"Harper shared it with me two weeks ago," Uncle Kevin said. "But I still haven't wrapped my head around how many fluky twists and coincidences had to have lined up for us to be here today."

Mr. Forester slipped off the neck strap of the apron and hung it over the chair arm. He looked toward the front window and beyond. "We have two mysteries on our hands."

"What do you mean?" Mateo asked.

"Where the hell was that nightstand for fifty-two years? And how did it get to the thrift store?"

"Thanks for putting that in my head, Gramps. You just gave me something new to obsess over for the rest of my life."

Laughter painted the living room with warmth. I felt like I belonged, like I was the reason this wonderful moment happened.

"So, getting back to Grams," Mateo said, still laughing. "Do you think it was her who set me and Harper up to meet?"

"I wouldn't put it past her," Mr. Forester said.

"I wish I could have met her," I said, with a genuine sense of attachment.

Mr. Forester's voice carried the weight of all the years he had lived when he said, "I think you did. Libby believed in affirmations, and the power of positive thinking, and a world beyond imagination. I wouldn't be surprised if she drummed this up." He gave me a thoughtful smile. "One thing she liked to say was, 'What's meant to be always finds its way.'"

An endless sense of love and gratitude filled me. I thought of Mama. She would have called it happiness.

ACKNOWLEDGMENTS:

Writing a novel is a solitary undertaking, and in the throes of a Pandemic, even more so. I'm fortunate to be surrounded by talented and multi-faceted support groups that I think of as a kaleidoscope of enlightened souls.

The friendship and encouragement I got from my eclectic friends in the Chicka Chicka Boom Writers Group has helped light my journey.

I'm grateful for the talented ladies in "The Quartet," whose finely tuned observations have been discerning and spot-on.

I thank the exceptional writers who invited me to join their Chautaugus Critique Group. Their thoughts have been invaluable.

Then, there are the brave ones, the true foot soldiers, my "First Readers," who endured clumsy, early drafts and whose input helped immensely.

I am especially grateful for my writing family at the Santa Barbara Writers Conference, where, as a fledgling writer, I was accepted with open arms. It's the same SBWC where I now teach a workshop.

My admiration for social activist Kipp Dawson is immense. Kipp's vision for a better world and steadfast commitment to social justice for over sixty years inspired the character of Kate Lawson.

And thank you to the talented graphic artist, Ron Larson, for the cover design.

# Book Club Discussion Questions

1.  Ordinary people can make a change is one of the themes that runs through this story. Can you think of others? How were those themes brought to life?

2.  How thought-provoking did you find this book?

3.  Which scene has stuck with you the most? Who was your favorite character and why?

4.  In what ways did the diary serve as a guide to Harper?

5.  What do you think would have happened to Libby if she had stayed in North Forks?

6.  How do you feel about the role of social activism in our country?

7. How well did the author blend historical facts and fiction in this book?

8. If you could talk to the author, what is your number one question for her?

www.nancyklann-moren.com,
klanncy@aol.com

Made in the USA
Las Vegas, NV
20 May 2024

89935049R00177